"Very well-done. I like your style, Peggy Dean."

"Yours has improved upon acquaintance," Peggy retorted lightly to Adam's compliment. "I nearly died when you chose me."

"A matter of self-preservation. The other two would've eaten me for dinner."

"It must be sickening to be so sexy," she mocked. "But you consented to it."

"Another night, another woman. What's the difference?" Adam muttered cynically.

"Really!" Peggy glared with hostility at the all-too-handsome face. "I hereby renounce my prize, Adam Gale! You're free of any obligations, and furthermore, you can go to hell!"

"And just who the hell do you think you are?" Adam glared, his pride obviously wounded.

"The woman with a difference!" Peggy snapped back.

Damn him! No
this much befo

Emma Darcy nearly became an actress until her fiancé declared he preferred to attend the theater *with* her. She became a wife and mother. Later she took up oil painting—unsuccessfully, she remarks. Then, she tried architecture, designing the family home in New South Wales. Next came romance writing—"the hardest and most challenging of all the activities," she confesses.

Books by Emma Darcy

Blind Date

Emma Darcy

Harlequin Books

TORONTO • NEW YORK • LONDON
AMSTERDAM • PARIS • SYDNEY • HAMBURG
STOCKHOLM • ATHENS • TOKYO • MILAN

Original hardcover edition published in 1986
by Mills & Boon Limited

ISBN 0-373-02900-4

Harlequin Romance first edition April 1988

CHAPTER ONE

'I RECOGNISE that smug look, Peggy Dean. So what have you won this time?'

Peggy glanced up from the official letter she had been reading. Her lively brown eyes sparkled with triumph, but she gave vent to a vexed sigh as she saw that Gavin had helped himself to a glass of milk and the last apple from her fruit basket.

'Next time you come home with me to work on an assignment, you can bring your own food with you, Gavin Howes.'

He pulled a face of injured innocence. 'You'd begrudge me a little snack? Here I am, prepared to share my genius with you . . .'

'You're here to pick my brains, not my pantry,' she flashed back at him.

'You owe me this in transport costs,' he argued and munched into the apple.

Peggy grudgingly conceded the point. Gavin lived in Glebe, within walking distance of The Institute where they were both students. The fare to and from Neutral Bay was more than the price of an apple, but they both knew that the terrace house he shared with four other students afforded little privacy for serious work. Peggy's bedsitter was always the venue for such get-togethers and Gavin invariably set about ruining her food budget. However, right at this moment, her pleasure at the news she had just received overrode her irritation.

'I've won myself a really good stereo set, the complete collection of Adam Gale's records, plus two free tickets to *Blind Date*. How about that?' she crowed.

Gavin cocked his head on one side and pursed his lips appreciatively. 'Not bad. Wouldn't mind seeing that musical. You can take me.'

'Mmh . . . maybe.' Her eyes skimmed the second page which outlined what was required of her to fulfil the terms of the competition. The third page was an acceptance form which had to be signed and returned. 'It'll be interesting to get a background view of how the Ross Elliot Show works too,' she mused.

'Oh? How does that come into it?'

Gavin's interest was suddenly very much alive. Both he and Peggy were majoring in audio-visual communication and vying for top honours in their last year of study. The skills and techniques involved in the planning and production of radio, film and television programmes were therefore of vital interest, and any first-hand experience with a top-rating television show had to be advantageous.

'I'll be going on the show,' Peggy answered smugly.

'What? To pick up the prizes?' Gavin scoffed as if such an appearance was of little consequence.

'In a way.'

'What way?' he demanded sharply, niggled into open curiosity.

Peggy gave him a teasing grin and handed him the letter to read, extracting only the acceptance form which she proceeded to fill in. Gavin flopped on to the sofa, shoved a pillow under his head and generally made himself comfortable. Peggy had the form signed and sealed in an envelope before he had finished reading. She slipped into the kitchenette to get a glass of water then propped herself against the archway leading into the living-room and watched Gavin's face with some amusement.

Gavin gave everything he read intense concentration. He was an intense young man; clever, ambitious, and very, very competitive. There was no doubt in Peggy's mind that he would forge a successful path somewhere in the communications field. He had one advantage over Peggy; he was male. But she hoped that her own abilities and high qualifications would outweigh the disadvantage of being female when it came to seeking a job.

She liked Gavin, despite his irritating habit of assuming he could make himself at home with anything in her home. They enjoyed matching wits with each other, but neither of them had any inclination to take their relationship beyond a platonic friendship. Gavin relished the role of master and he knew perfectly well that Peggy would never wear the role of submissive disciple. It always amazed her that so many girls were attracted to him, since he treated them all with a kind of casual contempt.

Physically he was not particularly attractive. He was thin and gangly despite his habit of continually fuelling his body. His face was also thin and his bushy brown hair made it look thinner. He had a longish nose and a full-lipped, rather sensual mouth. His eyes were his most striking feature, challenging green eyes which always seemed to be wickedly provocative. Peggy supposed it was these, along with his sharp mind and facile tongue, that gave him the power to be the dominant figure among the students in their faculty. Dominant except for Peggy, to whom he grudgingly acknowledged almost equal status.

He suddenly shot a hard, speculative look at her. 'You're really going through with this, Peggy?'

She shrugged. 'Why not?'

He pursed his mouth. 'Didn't think a rabid feminist would compete for a date with a pop-star.'

An indignant flush swept into Peggy's cheeks. 'Point one . . . I am not a rabid feminist. Point two . . . I am not competing for a date with Adam Gale.'

Gavin's mouth twisted with mockery. 'Come on, Peggy. The label fits. You've got a body which screams sex, but I bet you've never had it off with anyone. And you know why? Because you intimidate every guy you meet with your competitiveness. You want to be a better man than he is, all the time scoring points. You never switch off your mind long enough to let yourself be a woman.'

The flush burnt to an angry red. 'What's a woman to you, Gavin? A soft, cuddly, convenient body? I happen to want a man who turns me on in every department, and I don't think that makes me any less of a woman,' she bit out scornfully.

'No?' His eyebrows arched in teasing mockery. 'Well, correct me if I'm wrong, but as one of the three chosen finalists of this competition, you will be lined up on the Ross Elliot Show, and Adam

Gale is to choose one of you as his blind date.'

'That's right. One of us. And the losers get the consolation of the prizes listed in the letter. I intend to be a loser.'

'You, a loser? Peggy Dean a loser?' Gavin rolled around in fits of laughter.

'I'll win what I want to win,' Peggy retorted tersely, and walked over to snatch the letter out of his hand. Somehow Gavin had soured her triumph with his mockery and she was thoroughly annoyed with him, particularly over his suggestion that she was unfeminine. While she believed in equal rights and equal opportunities for both sexes, that did not make her a *rabid* feminist. And as for sex, she could see no point in sharing her bed and body with someone she did not particularly want. The very thought caused her nose to wrinkle with distaste.

Gavin was hugging himself with glee and his eyes sparkled with devilish mischief. 'I hate to contradict you, Peggy, but it's Adam Gale in control of the winning and losing. And my bet is, he'll see you as the most promising candidate for his bed, God help him!' He burst into another peal of laughter, spitting out words in hysterical amusement. 'I can see it now . . . him wanting a roll in the hay, and you on your high-horse. Oh God! I wish I could be a fly on the wall.'

Peggy adopted a pose of haughty disdain. 'I am not amused, Gavin, and for your information, he does not get a look at the contestants. It's a blind date. Blind, as in not able to see. The whole thing is a publicity gimmick for this musical he's starring in. He is to ask each contestant a series of questions and he has to choose from the answers given. I don't think he's going to like my answers.'

Gavin's grin turned into an expressive grimace. 'Pity! You would have been one hell of an experience for Adam Gale. He's probably never been knocked back in his life. Must have a king-size ego, that guy. All those groupies hanging around in panting adoration.'

'Precisely why I wouldn't want his company, even for one night. Much as I like Adam Gale's music, the man's attitude to women is sure to be insufferable,' Peggy commented acidly.

Gavin's grin was back. 'Feminist! And one of these days, Peggy Dean, you're going to be caught short of an answer. I wonder what you'll do then.'

'Nothing, until I think of one,' she answered flippantly. 'Did you remember to bring the book of plays?'

'Have you ever known me to forget anything?' he retorted with typical arrogance.

Peggy grinned. 'One of these days you will, and I wonder what you'll do. Come on. Let's get down to work.'

No more was said about the *Blind Date* competition until the assignment had been completed and Gavin was packing up to go home.

'You know, Peggy, you ought to try winning that date. Adam Gale probably knows a lot of influential people in television. It could be handy to cultivate his acquaintance.'

She arched a mocking eyebrow at him. 'I don't intend to sleep my way to success.'

He shook his head. 'You really are a dumb broad

in some respects. Sex is power.'

'Everything's power to you, Gavin.'

He grinned. 'Too right it is. You could learn from me, Peggy.'

'No, thanks. I'll make it my own way.'

He hoisted his bag over his shoulder, walked to the door and opened it before delivering his parting shot. 'I don't believe you've ever made it.'

His swift exit denied her a retort but she was relieved not to have to think of one. Although she would never admit it to him, Gavin had hit on the truth. She had never felt the slightest desire to abandon herself to any of her boyfriends' lovemaking and she was still a virgin—a fact that Gavin would use for unmerciful teasing if she ever revealed it.

Other girls seemed to fall in and out of love with monotonous regularity. Peggy had concluded that they were more in love with the idea than any actual man, but now she wondered if she had merely been excusing her own inability to become emotionally involved. It was a worrisome thought.

Here she was, twenty-one years old, and not one man had caused a flutter in her heart. Was it a fault in her that she had never been moved to romanticise the opposite sex? Most other girls she knew papered the walls of their living quarters with posters of pop-stars or television heroes. Her walls displayed prints of Vlaminck and Derain, bold splashes of flaming colour by the leading artists of the Fauves movement. They gave her far more pleasure than the paper-faces of celebrities. All the same, she did seem to be out of step with the norm in her age-group.

But she was not, definitely not, a rabid feminist. And the same thought echoed in her mind ten days later as she stood in front of her mirror and approved her reflection. Gavin's claim was just plain ridiculous. She liked dressing up and looking her feminine best and had no inclination to be the least bit mannish.

The dark red filmy blouse was the essence of femininity with its deeply frilled neckline, and she loved the black velvet skirt over which she had spent hours sewing a patterned border of thin, dark red ribbon above the hemline. The sheer black stockings and black suede high-heels added elegance to what she considered was a very classy outfit. In fact, it was with some regret that she donned her black and white houndstooth overcoat, but it was still winter and the August wind was cold.

Luckily the wind would have no detrimental effect on her hairstyle. Nothing ever did: wind, sun or rain. The tight black ringlets which framed her face and dangled down to her shoulders were always the same neat—tidy, uncontrollably bent on having their own way. Her pale-skinned oval face required little make-up and Peggy had only applied lipstick. Her brown eyes were thickly fringed and her eyebrows naturally arched, and she figured it was better to leave any more make-up to the studio beautician who was especially skilled at the job.

Pride had dictated that she look her best for this appearance on national television. Since her parents and their friends would be watching the Ross

Elliot Show, she wanted them to be proud of her. A smile curved the perfectly shaped mouth as she remembered her father's gusts of laughter when she had explained her plan to avoid being chosen as Adam Gale's date.

Her smile turned into a grimace as she then recalled her mother's reaction. Her mother had not been amused. Her mother could not understand why Peggy did not want to spend a romantic evening with such a handsome, talented man, but then Marjorie Dean had never come to grips with the modern generation.

Peggy had been born when her mother was forty and her father fifty, and nothing her mother had ever told her about men had had any relevance at all to the society in which Peggy moved. Her father, although older, was far more aware of the changes in social and sexual mores. He had always encouraged Peggy to be her own person and not look to a man to supply her needs, because these days too many marriages were not forever. He had nurtured in her the independence of mind and spirit required of a survivor.

Her father's advice had always made good sense to Peggy and she was determined to follow it. And that didn't make her a feminist either, she insisted to herself as she locked the door of her bedsitter behind her. It was her actual femininity which bugged Gavin, not her supposed feminism.

Although the television studio was on the north side of Sydney Harbour, Peggy had to catch two different buses to get there from Neutral Bay where she lived. She had given herself plenty of time for

the trip and despite a long delay while she waited
for the second bus, it was still ten minutes short of
eleven o'clock when she arrived. Nevertheless, as
soon as she had given her name at the reception
desk she was escorted to a make-up room where a
beautician wasted no time in setting to work on her
face.

'Hmmm . . . you don't need much. Some colour to
highlight those cheekbones and a touch of shade to
the eyes. You're lucky to have so many natural
assets. Particularly the hair.'

The matter-of-fact comment was a judgement
rather than a compliment and the girl gave Peggy
no time for a reply.

She flashed a knowing grin. 'Feeling excited?'

'A little,' Peggy admitted. Appearing on the Ross
Elliot Show was hardly an everyday occurrence.

The grin widened. 'Well, good luck to you. Pity
it's a blind date. Bet he'd pick you out of a line-up.'

Peggy grimaced at the thought. 'I wouldn't be
here if it was a line-up.'

Eyebrows shot up. 'Really? I'd line up for Adam
Gale any day. In fact I have in years gone by, when
he used to give concerts. Camped out all one night,
and I got tickets in the front row too. That was
really something! Ever seen him perform live?'

'No.'

'Wow! You don't know what you've missed. I
almost fainted from sheer excitement. My heart was
pumping like crazy. The music and the voice and
the man himself . . . as I said, wow!'

The door opened and another girl was ushered in.
She had almost waist-length, ash-blonde hair and

was dressed to kill in a slinky, blue-knit dress which was so tight that the line of her panties showed. Her blue eyes had been given the Cleopatra treatment, wildly elongated and colour to the eyebrows.

The beautician sighed and waved her to a chair. 'You can take Miss Dean now,' she said to the woman who had accompanied the girl.

'Good!' the woman nodded. 'Miss Dean, this is Miss Merrill. Our third contestant has not yet arrived but no doubt you'll both be meeting her soon.'

Peggy smiled politely at the other girl, but the painted blue eyes measured her with cold hostility. The beautician whipped off the plastic cape which had protected Peggy's clothes. She was free to leave and quite happy to go. Miss Merrill clearly considered Peggy an opponent with whom she had no intention of being friendly.

'Would it be possible for me to watch the technicians at work for a while?' Peggy asked her usherette as she was led along a corridor. 'I won't get in their way. I'm studying audio-visual communication and . . .'

'No. Quite impossible,' the woman cut in curtly. 'The three of you are to be shut in a waiting-room so that there's no possibility of your being seen by Adam Gale.' She glanced at her watch. 'He's due at the studio at eleven-forty-five and we can't risk any hitches.'

Peggy resigned herself to the disappointment. After all, she was here for the competition and had to abide by the rules.

The waiting-room was very pleasant. Several

armchairs were grouped around a table on which stood a delightful arrangement of flowers. A magazine rack held a number of glossy publications and a drinks table held ample provisions for the thirsty. A television set was switched on to the current affairs programme which preceded the Ross Elliot Show but its volume was turned down low.

'You'll be collected at twelve-thirty. Just relax and make yourself comfortable, Miss Dean,' was the woman's parting advice.

Peggy selected a fashion magazine to flick through and settled into one of the armchairs. It was not long before the sexy blonde was ushered into the room, teetering on the highest heels Peggy had ever seen. Once they had been left together the blonde headed straight for the drinks and poured herself a neat shot of vodka. The make-up around the blue eyes had been considerably toned down and to Peggy's mind, the girl looked much better. She was undeniably pretty and her figure was certainly eye-catching. Sex-kitten on the prowl, Peggy thought with sly amusement, and she probably wants to scratch my eyes out.

'How old are you?' the girl suddenly challenged, once again measuring Peggy for competition.

'Twenty-one,' she answered readily.

'You don't look it.' The remark was almost sneered.

Peggy shrugged. 'Oh, I daresay my age will catch up with me some day.' Her gaze dropped pointedly to the glass of hard liquor. 'Are you nervous?'

The girl took a defiant swallow of her drink

before replying. 'Aren't you?'

'Not particularly.'

'It'll catch up with you,' came the mocking retort. 'I'm settling my stomach before we go on.'

'Yes, well, that's probably a good idea,' Peggy said off-handedly and started turning the pages of her magazine. The tone of the conversation was not to her liking.

'Did you do your own writing?'

'Pardon?'

The blonde spelled it out as if Peggy was a dimwit. 'You know. The twenty-five words that got us here.'

'Oh yes. Yes I did.'

'Clever, are you?'

Peggy shrugged. 'Not bad with words.'

'I got a friend in advertising to write mine. He's a whiz at jingles.' The smugness in her voice showed a complete disregard for the fact that she had cheated.

Peggy dropped her gaze to the magazine again, pointedly discouraging further talk. She had just found an interesting article when the door opened to admit the third contestant.

'This is Miss Wilson. Miss Dean, Miss Merrill,' came the efficient introduction from the woman who had not bothered to introduce herself. 'I'll collect you when it's time to move,' she added and shut the door again.

The newcomer glanced admiringly from Peggy to the blonde and a huge grin spread across her face. 'Oh boy! I'm sure glad he won't be able to see us or I'd be sunk. The name is Amy, by the way.'

Peggy smiled an immediate response to the
vivacious good humour of the girl. 'Hello, Amy. I'm
Peggy.'

'Marilyn,' the blonde pouted.

Peggy almost giggled.

Amy did. The girl's humour was obviously
irrepressible. She held out her arms in a pose which
revealed little shape under the fashionable green
and camel shift. 'If only I'd been christened
Marilyn, maybe I would've grown curves in all the
right places. What I'd do for an hour-glass figure
like yours!'

Marilyn preened, and Peggy grinned.

Amy flopped her beanpole frame into an arm-
chair and gave an exaggerated sigh. 'Well, I'm here.
And that's something of a miracle. At the very least
I'll get to meet that dream of a man.'

Peggy had to laugh at the fatuous look on Amy's
face. It could not be called a pretty face with its
bumpy nose and crooked mouth, but it was made
remarkably attractive by the personality which
shone through.

'It's all right for you,' Amy chided her good-
naturedly. 'I bet you have good-looking guys around
you all the time. This is my one chance at a real
jackpot.' She eyed Peggy's black curls with envy.
'That's not permed hair, is it?'

'No, I've been cursed since birth.'

'Cursed!' Amy rolled her eyes. 'Would that I'd
been cursed like that!'

'You have lovely hair,' Peggy insisted. And it
was; thick, shiny brown and done in a soft, flyaway
style which suited her.

'Huh! It takes half an hour with a blow-dryer to achieve this effect. I'll probably end up with tendonitis in my right arm, all for the sake of vanity. I bet you two don't appreciate how lucky you are.'

Amy rattled on, talking non-stop, firing questions and making amusing little comments on their answers. Peggy wondered if it was her way of easing nervous tension but she was glad of the girl's company. The time passed quickly and pleasantly.

When the Ross Elliot Show came on at noon Marilyn turned up the volume on the television set. It was basically a chat show, interspersed with entertainment segments from visiting show-business personalities. The first guest was a well-known astrologer, Victor Renshaw. He was a good showman, entertaining the audience with his subject. He had the air of a professor with his gold-rimmed glasses and goatee-beard.

'Do you follow your stars, Peggy?' Amy asked.

'No. A lot of nonsense, isn't it?' she retorted drily.

'I don't know about that. I was reading . . .'

'Shush!' Marilyn hissed and frowned at both of them.

Amy sighed and Peggy gave her a commiserating smile as they obliged Marilyn with silence.

'I believe you've done Adam Gale's horoscope, Victor,' Ross Elliot was saying, his jovial, boy-next-door face alive with interest.

'Yes. He's a Leo, you know,' came the dry answer.

Ross Elliot laughed. 'I should have known. He's certainly the lion of the pop-jungle.'

'Since the sun is Leo's ruler, it's not surprising

that Adam should shine in his chosen sphere, but I believe he would in any field. Leos are born to command.'

'What other characteristics do they have?' Ross Elliot encouraged, sending a cheeky grin to the studio audience as he whispered in an aside, 'I'm a Leo.'

Victor gave a broad smile. 'Oh, they're proud, arrogant, vain . . .'

'That's enough!' Ross howled in protest, much to the audience's amusement.

Victor laughed and continued, 'They're also warm, generous, strong, protective and loving.'

'Ah! That's more like it,' Ross declared with a smug look which raised laughter from the crowd. He paused to allow the noise to drop then climbed to his feet and held out a welcoming arm. 'I hope you heard that, Adam. Victor's been giving away our secrets.'

'Not too many, I trust,' came the beautifully modulated voice of Adam Gale.

He strolled on to the set, acknowledged the applause of the audience with a royal wave, shook hands with the two men, and made himself comfortable in the armchair provided. He wore a conservatively tailored, dark grey lounge-suit and looked like any woman's dream come true.

He was, without a doubt, the most attractive male on the pop-scene. No garish make-up for him. No weird hairstyle or outlandish costume: he had a face and body which carried their own powerful impact. Quite simply he was stunningly handsome.

The bone-structure of his face was distinctly

masculine, clear-cut, hard and striking, like a strong piece of sculpture. The rather deep-set eyes were an intense blue, a sharp contrast to his dark olive skin and black hair which was thick and straight, layered to shape his head and cut to collar-length.

'Oh, I could drown in those eyes,' Amy sighed.

Peggy threw her a smile, but she was too interested in the conversation on the show to encourage Amy to more comment. Ross Elliot was drawing Adam Gale out about the musical, *Blind Date*. '. . . so basically it's the old Cinderella story?'

'But very much in the modern idiom. Billy Prince is a pop-star and Cindy Jones is the average working-girl, and the story revolves around a number of today's social issues. *West Side Story* modernised *Romeo and Juliet* very successfully and believe me, *Blind Date* is just as dramatic and emotional.'

Adam Gale spoke with convincing eloquence and Peggy was impressed. Not smitten, but impressed. The man spoke as well as he sang.

Ross Elliot nodded as if he were impressed too. 'You must be very pleased with the resounding success of the theme song.'

'Yes, it's very encouraging.'

'You wrote that one yourself, didn't you?'

'Yes, that one's mine. As you know, I collaborated with Jenny Ross on the score. She wrote Cindy's songs and we worked out the duets between us.'

'Jenny Ross has written some great music.'

'She's a wonderful person,' Adam Gale said with obvious warmth. 'I've learnt a great deal from her.'

Ross Elliot raised questioning eyebrows. 'I

thought *Blind Date* carried more emotion than you usually put in your songs. Her influence?'

Adam Gale laughed. 'I'm not incapable of emotion, Ross.'

'Well, Adam, there are three young ladies who are probably feeling very emotional about meeting you very shortly. How do you feel about your blind date? Are you like Billy Prince in the musical, looking for true romance?'

A little smile played around Adam Gale's mouth. 'One can but hope.'

Ross Elliot grinned. 'Have you worked out the questions you're going to ask?'

'Oh yes.' The blue eyes danced with devilment.

'Well now, we're going to put your video of *Blind Date* on the screen and while our viewers are enjoying . . .'

The door to the waiting-room was abruptly opened and the woman who had taken charge of them before, beckoned them out. 'Time to go, girls.'

CHAPTER TWO

THE three girls rose to their feet. Amy took a deep breath and waggled her eyebrows at Peggy, and Marilyn licked her lips and practised a wiggle. Peggy felt the surge of adrenalin which always sharpened her mind when there was a challenge to be met.

'Now, please don't speak when I'm positioning you on the set,' their instructress warned. 'Miss Merrill, you will be contestant number one, Miss Wilson, number two, and Miss Dean, number three. You will be referred to by number during the questions so that complete anonymity is retained until Mr Gale chooses his date. Please remember your number. Now follow me.'

They were led straight across the corridor and through a doorway which led directly onto the set. It surprised Peggy that they had been so close to it all the time. Three beautifully carved Louis XIV chairs stood in a row to one side of a screen which was obviously blocking off the Ross Elliot grouping on the other side.

Marilyn Merrill was placed in the chair closest to the screen, Amy in the middle, and then Peggy. When they were all seated the woman stepped back, signalled their readiness and withdrew. Amy rolled her eyes at Peggy and lifted crossed fingers. Peggy smiled at her, hoping she would win the date,

although someone like Marilyn was probably more
to Adam Gale's taste.

'One can but hope.' The arrogant condescension
of those words raised Peggy's hackles. She had
never given any weight to astrology but Victor
Renshaw's first summary of a Leo seemed an apt
description for a man like Adam Gale: proud,
arrogant, vain. It would do him good to be pulled
down a peg or two. Peggy sharpened her mind with
secret relish. If he thought all three of them were
hanging breathlessly on his decision, he was in for a
little surprise.

The video of the song had come to an end. Ross
Elliot's voice carried over the screen. 'Well, Adam,
one of the girls behind that screen will be your blind
date. Our viewers can see them now but I will leave
the introductions until after you've made your
choice. We will simply refer to them as contestants
number one, two and three. Each contestant will
answer the same question in turn. Will you ask your
first question now of number one?'

There was barely a pause. 'Number one, what is
your opinion of men's liberation?' The tone was
amused, almost mocking.

Marilyn drew a deep breath and her voice took on
a husky purr. 'I'm all for it. I love liberated men.
They're so much more exciting than the squares and
it's a lot more interesting for a woman, not knowing
what to expect from them.'

The audience buzzed with muted comment.

'Number two?' Adam Gale asked, not giving
anything away.

Amy burst into a torrent of words. 'I think

everyone should be liberated from standard roles. They should be free to take on whatever role brings them the most satisfaction, and it shouldn't be judged as wrong or unsuitable just because you're a man or woman.'

There was a smattering of applause from the audience and Amy flushed with gratification.

'Mmmh . . . and number three?'

Peggy barely suppressed a grin. 'I'm dead against it. I think men should be kept barefoot and pregnant and in the kitchen where they belong.'

There was a concerted gasp around the studio, followed by a ripple of laughter.

'Does that put you in your place, Adam?' came Ross Elliot's amused comment.

'The pregnant part does present some difficulty,' was the very dry answer.

The audience roared with laughter.

'Do I take it you don't favour number three's answer?' Ross enquired.

'I found each answer very interesting. However, I would have to agree with the principles stated by number two. I don't believe one should be forced by social standards into roles which are constricting.'

Peggy had to confess herself surprised by Adam Gale's acceptance of Amy's rather philosophical answer. The man was not as superficial as she had thought. She smiled across at Amy, whose face was aglow with excitement. Marilyn's mouth was tight with frustration. Peggy relaxed. One successfully down. Two more questions to sabotage.

'So you'd choose number two on this answer,' Ross Elliot concluded.

'I agree with her answer,' came the non-committal reply.

'You're being very cagey, Adam.'

'Don't commit me to a choice until I've made it,' was the light retort.

'Uh-huh. Well, let's proceed to the next question. Please address it in the order of two, three and one.'

'Number two, how would you make the man in your life feel special?'

Amy opened her mouth, swallowed, and turned a blank look at Peggy, obviously frozen on an answer.

'Number two?' Ross Elliot urged.

'I'd give him a big hug and tell him I love him,' Amy rattled out at top speed.

The audience murmured approval.

'Number three?'

Peggy had never felt calmer. 'Absolutely nothing. I wouldn't respect a man who needs a girl to prop up his ego and make him feel special.'

There was a short silence. Peggy hoped it was the kind of silence which follows a neat punch in the gut.

'Number one?'

Marilyn threw Peggy a scornful glance and purred into her sex-kitten act. 'I'd pamper him in every way possible. I'd learn whatever he enjoyed most and do it for him whenever he wanted.'

No one was left in any doubt as to what Marilyn meant. Her voice promised everything: slave, geisha-girl and doormat, all rolled up together. Peggy was disgusted, but undoubtedly it would be precisely what Adam Gale wanted.

'And which of those answers struck your fancy,

Adam?' Ross Elliot quizzed.

Adam Gale laughed, a deep attractive rumble of
amusement. 'I don't think there's a man alive who
could turn his back on number one's answer.'

Peggy felt a smug glow of satisfaction at the
confirmation of her judgement. The sinuous squirm
of Marilyn's body was smug too; she had succeeded
in impressing her quarry. Amy's face was slightly
crestfallen. Peggy gave her a cheer-up smile. There
was still another question for Amy to catch up lost
ground. Peggy wondered where the best place
would be for her new stereo-set.

'And now the last question,' Ross Elliot drawled,
building up suspense. 'Direct it first to number
three, Adam, then one and two.'

'Number three, what is the biggest thing in
making a perfect marriage?'

A titter ran around the audience, but Peggy was
not amused by the sexual innuendo.

'Recognising the fact that no-one is perfect,' she
whipped back with pointed emphasis. And that
should completely wipe me out of contention, she
thought, well-pleased with the negative impact of
all her answers.

'Number one?'

Marilyn came in on cue, almost panting with
eagerness. 'A great sex-life. If you're satisfied in bed
then the rest will fall into place.'

The predictable answer drew predictable grins
from the audience.

'Number two?'

Amy heaved a sigh and answered in a tone which
was already resigned to defeat. 'Well, if we're

assuming that love is already there, I think a shared sense of humour is important.'

'I'd agree with that,' Ross Elliot said in his droll way, 'but it's not for me to say. What say you, Adam?'

'Oh, I'd definitely agree that a shared sense of humour is important . . .'

Amy perked up.

'And I can't imagine a marriage being perfect without a great sex-life . . .'

The pleasure on Amy's face dimmed as Marilyn took on the expression of a cat who had cornered the cream market.

'But without the tolerance which comes from accepting that neither partner is perfect, I can't believe that a marriage would be workable, let alone perfect.'

Peggy froze. She didn't like the sound of that. Surely he was not giving preference to her answer, an answer which had been specifically designed to mock his vanity? Had she miscalculated the man?

'Ah, you're indeed a showman, Adam, keeping us all in suspense to the last moment,' Ross Elliot crooned appreciatively. 'One approval for each number gives us no hint of your final choice.'

Of course! A showman holding his audience! Peggy breathed a sigh of relief. No way would she be the final choice. The stereo-set was as good as in her living-room.

Ross Elliot burbled on. 'You have a few moments now to ponder all those answers and come to your decision. I'm going to ask Victor to note down the number he thinks you'll choose. An astrologer who has studied your stars should have some glimmering of the way your mind works and we'll just see how accurate Victor can be. Are you confident, Victor?'

'Reasonably so. Of course, Adam may choose uncharacteristically, just to confound me.'

'I assure you, Victor, my mind is definitely set on one of the ladies behind the screen,' Adam Gale declared.

'I thought it would be,' Victor Renshaw remarked knowingly. 'Here you are, Ross. You can hold the note. If I'm wrong I'll do you a free horoscope.'

'Is it written in the stars that Adam should meet his fate here today with this blind date?' Ross asked jokingly.

'That's up to him,' Victor replied. 'The signs are propitious.'

'How verrry, verrry interesting,' Ross rolled out with relish. 'Your time is up, Adam. Name your choice.'

Peggy looked across at Amy and Marilyn, curious to see their reaction. Their bodies tensed as they waited for the fateful words to be spoken.

'I must say I enjoyed the uninhibited answers of number one . . .'

Marilyn bounced in her seat.

Amy slumped.

'But then I appreciated very much the thoughtfulness and warmth exhibited by number two's answers . . .'

Marilyn threw a vexed grimace at Amy who beamed with a new lease of life.

'If the choice were between those two ladies, it

would be a very difficult one, but I find myself totally intrigued with number three. So I choose number three as my blind date.'

CHAPTER THREE

THREE? Had he really said three? Peggy couldn't believe her ears, but Amy and Marilyn were looking at her, Amy with envy, Marilyn with venom. How could he have said three? What on earth had possessed him to say three? How dared he say three!

She had made it perfectly plain she didn't want to be chosen. Mutiny stirred in her heart. She would decline. The thought of Gavin crowing over her error of judgement was intolerable. And damn, damn, damn! She was going to miss out on the stereo-set.

Could she decline the date? No, she had signed the acceptance form and good faith demanded that she go along with the outcome of the competition. *But it wasn't what I planned*, she wailed in silent frustration.

The studio audience was applauding enthusiastically as if Adam Gale's choice had been a popular one. Peggy shook her head in bewilderment. Everyone was mad. She was no match for him. Couldn't they see that? The whole thing was ridiculous! And embarrassing. Why, oh why had Adam Gale been so perverse as to choose her?

'Well, Adam, the moment of truth approaches,' Ross Elliot drawled provocatively. 'However, before I introduce you to your blind date, I'd like you to meet the other two young ladies. Number one is a professional dancer, Miss Marilyn Merrill. Miss Merrill, will you please step around the screen?'

Marilyn undulated out of sight and the whistles and roar from the crowd indicated that Adam Gale had not been greeted by a demure handshake. Peggy's stomach curled into a knot. She hoped that Adam Gale did not assume that she would want a public cuddle.

'Thank you, Miss Merrill,' Ross Elliot said in a bemused tone. 'Ummm . . . a bit of lipstick there, Adam. Right. Number two is a schoolteacher, Miss Amy Wilson. Miss Wilson, will you now come around the screen?'

Amy stood up, mouthed 'good luck' to Peggy, gave a little 'oh well' shrug and went the way of Marilyn. The milder response from the crowd suggested that this meeting with Adam Gale was more restrained.

'Miss Merrill and Miss Wilson will be taking away with them a stereo-set from a well-known manufacturer, a complete collection of Adam's songs, and two free tickets to *Blind Date*. Thank you, ladies.' Ross Elliot's announcement was clearly a dismissal and the subsequent applause obviously punctuated Marilyn's and Amy's departure from the set. Peggy wished the floor would open and swallow her up; she could feel a tide of warmth creeping up her neck. The only remotely comforting thought was that her mother would be pleased.

'And now, Adam, your blind date. She is a student at the New South Wales Institute of Technology, and in her final year of a Bachelor of

Arts course which specialises in communication. Miss Peggy Dean, would you please come forward and meet Adam Gale.'

Peggy rose to her feet and to her horror, felt her knees turn to jelly. Gritting her teeth into a polite smile and sending a charge of will-power to her traitorous legs, she managed a dignified walk around the screen. Good God! Her heart was pounding. Or was it the beat of clapping hands in her ears?

Her step faltered as Adam Gale walked towards her. Did he have to be so tall and handsome? she thought wildly. The top of her head was about level with his chin, and Peggy was not short. In instinctive defence against the magnetic presence of the man, Peggy squared her shoulders and lifted her chin. His hands reached out as if to pull her into an embrace; her eyes flashed a vehement rejection as she thrust her own hand forward.

'How do you do, Mr Gale?' she clipped out with cool formality.

His smile held more than a quirk of amusement as he took her hand in both of his. 'I think I've done very well, Miss Dean,' he replied gravely, while the vivid blue eyes laughed outright.

It jolted her, that silent laughter. It was as if he were enjoying a huge joke and her cold handshake had been the punchline. Peggy's mind raced to compute the possibilities of the situation. She had underestimated the intelligence of the man, that was certain. He had guessed that she did not want to be his date. The knowledge was dancing in those eyes, knowledge confirmed beyond a doubt by her stiff greeting. So why had he picked her?

Ross Elliot descended on them with the benevolent smile of a fairy godfather who had brought lovers together. 'You two look very well-matched, if I may say so. I'd like you to come and sit down with Victor and myself. I'm sure our viewers are eager to learn more about the girl Adam has chosen for his date, Miss Peggy Dean.'

A burst of applause approved the move as Ross Elliot took Peggy's arm and led her to an armchair to the right of his. Victor Renshaw sat to the left of him and then Adam Gale. The chairs were placed in an arc so that when Peggy sat down she was virtually facing the man who had chosen her.

His gaze held hers for a moment, sharply speculative, then slowly and deliberately moved down to her feet and up again. With supreme disdain Peggy returned the physical appraisal, arching her eyebrows in mocking challenge when she finally lifted her gaze to his once again. The laughter was back, wild, rollicking laughter inviting her to be equally amused. A smile tugged at her mouth. Maybe it wouldn't be so bad, getting to know Adam Gale, she decided. It might even be fun. Arrogant he certainly was, but the mind inside the man was arousing her interest.

Ross Elliot had noted their mutual appraisal and asked, 'Have you ever seen Adam in the flesh before, Peggy?'

'No, only on television.'

'Does he seem any different to you here?'

'No. Except possibly taller than I had imagined.'

He turned to Adam Gale. 'When you made your

choice, did you envisage a girl as lovely as Peggy, Adam?'

'Yes.'

Ross looked surprised. 'What gave you that impression?'

The blue eyes twinkled knowingly at Peggy. 'Only a woman who's very confident of herself would have given such answers. In my experience, the kind of confidence Miss Dean displayed is always associated with natural beauty.'

'And did that sway your decision?' Ross Elliot asked interestedly.

'No, not at all. I felt Miss Dean and I would have a lot in common.'

Ross turned to her. 'And what about you, Peggy? Do you think you'd have a lot in common with Adam?'

'I don't know,' she answered slowly, watching his eyes for a reaction. 'But I'm curious to find out.'

The laughter was back. Adam Gale was thoroughly enjoying the situation. At her expense? Did it amuse him that she had been forced to take him instead of the stereo-set she wanted?

Ross Elliot switched to his other guest. 'Well, Victor, I have your note here. I'm sure the viewers would like to know if your prediction was correct.'

Victor Renshaw smiled. 'It was.'

Ross unfolded the note and held it up for the cameras. 'There it is. Number three.'. The studio audience applauded and Victor Renshaw took a bow which stirred more applause. 'Tell us how you knew,' Ross asked him as the buzz of appreciation subsided.

'To put it simply, Miss Dean threw out a challenge which no Leo would normally turn down. In fact, I shall be very surprised if Miss Dean is not an archer.'

'I assure you, Mr Renshaw, I've never taken up a bow and arrow in my life,' Peggy asserted firmly. And she hadn't been challenging Adam Gale either. The idea was absurd, as absurd, as all this astrology stuff which was a lot of bunkum.

'He means a Sagittarius,' Adam Gale commented drily

'Born between the twenty-third of November and the twenty-first of December,' Victor Renshaw elaborated.

'I'm sorry, I didn't realise what you meant,' Peggy said quickly, annoyed at being caught ignorant. 'Yes, I am a Sagittarius.'

'Strike up another point for you, Victor,' Ross said admiringly. 'And what led you to that conclusion?'

'The rebellious flavour of Miss Dean's first answer, the blunt candour of her second, and the clear perception of humanity contained in the third. Very typical of an archer.'

'Is that right?' Ross Elliot turned mischievous eyes to Peggy. 'Would you be completely candid if I asked what you felt when Adam chose you as his blind date?'

Annoyed by the astrologist's public analysis of her, Peggy did not seek a tactful answer. 'Frustrated!' she blurted out, throwing a defiant look at Adam Gale.

He threw back his head and gave vent to the

laughter he had been suppressing all along. Ross Elliot looked completely taken aback and Victor Renshaw sat there giving knowing little nods which irritated Peggy further.

'Well, there's candour, honesty and rebellion summed up in one word,' Adam Gale spluttered and made a visible effort to control himself. 'Tell me, Miss Dean, are you frequently frustrated?'

'Only when I lose, Mr Gale,' she shot back at him, resenting the sexual insinuation.

'But I don't understand, Peggy,' Ross Elliot intervened, 'you've won. Out of thousands of entries for this blind date, Adam chose you.'

She sighed, wishing now that she had held her tongue. It sounded as if she were putting down the aspirations of all the girls who had wanted Adam Gale's company for an evening, and that was not what she had intended at all.

'I didn't expect to win, Mr Elliot. I'm a student on a limited allowance, and I can't afford the luxuries of life. I was looking forward to owning a stereo-set. As much as I'm sure I'll enjoy a date with Mr Gale . . .' she flicked him a look of peace-making admiration, 'he's very handsome, very talented, and obviously has a charming sense of humour . . . nevertheless, it's only one date, while a stereo-set would have given me many more hours of pleasure.'

'Such devastating logic,' Victor Renshaw commented approvingly. 'An archer, right down the line.'

'Has Peggy shot an arrow into your heart, Adam?' Ross Elliot enquired, clearly at a loss with the situation.

'I am more delighted with Miss Dean every minute,' he answered good-humouredly. 'So delighted, in fact, that I hope she'll accept a stereo-set as a gift from me. I understand exactly how she feels. Music is my life and I would hate not to be able to play it whenever I liked.'

'That's very generous of you, Adam,' Ross commented.

'Typical of a Leo,' Victor Renshaw chimed in.

'I can't possibly accept it from you, Mr Gale,' Peggy said decisively.

'Why not?' he retorted. 'I deprived you of one.'

'Not by the rules of the competition. I've won a date with you, and that's that.'

His mouth curved into a whimsical smile. 'Oh, I wouldn't say that's that. There was no rule which stated there could not be more than one date.'

'Really, Mr Gale,' Peggy huffed, 'you're assuming an inclination on my part.'

'Oh boy!' Ross Elliot breathed and covered his eyes with his hand before leaning towards Victor Renshaw and saying in a theatrical aside, 'Have we a love match here or a combat?'

'What we have here are the competitive sparks which fly when two fire signs meet,' came the assured reply.

Ross looked alarmed. 'Should we expect a conflagration?'

The audience tittered.

'You don't understand, Ross. Miss Dean and Adam are enjoying themselves. Miss Dean is saying exactly what she pleases and Adam is countering her at every turn. I have no doubt that both of them are feeling quite exhilarated.'

'Do you mean this isn't a fight?'

Laughter broke out around the studio.

Adam Gale held his hands up in a gesture of limpid innocence. 'I'm not fighting.'

'And I'm just setting him straight,' Peggy pointed out matter-of-factly.

'Nothing like getting things straight,' agreed Adam.

Peggy turned on him. 'I'm glad you said that because I'd like to hear it straight from you why you chose me when you knew I didn't want to be chosen.'

'I really am sorry about the stereo. Please change your mind and let me give it to you.'

'You're evading my question.'

'So I am.'

'You see, Ross? Natural empathy,' Victor Renshaw commented smugly. 'The influence of the 5-9 Sun-Sign Pattern.'

Ross Elliot shook his head. 'You mean this blind date might actually work for these two?'

'They are compatible.'

Ross gestured an appeal to the studio audience. 'Do you believe that?'

'Yes!' they chorused back.

'They're not even calling each other by their Christian names.'

'Go on, Adam, call her Peggy,' urged someone in the audience.

'She might shoot me down,' he retorted in mock fear, as much a showman as Ross Elliot.

'Call him Adam, Peggy,' another suggested.

'Mr Gale, do you want me to call you Adam?' Peggy asked with arch politeness, not averse to joining in on the act.

'I think it would be a sign of friendliness,' he replied gravely. 'Might I be so boldly familiar as to call you Peggy?'

She burst out laughing. He had topped her on that one all right. The whole studio rocked with laughter.

'Good on you, Adam. Give it back to her,' some chauvinistic male advised.

'Keep him in line, Peggy. That's the way,' a female countered.

A shower of conflicting comments and advice was shouted from the audience until Ross Elliot stood up and gestured for silence and the hubbub gradually subsided.

'Right!' he nodded. 'I can see we have a serious conflict here. How would you like it if we set up combat zones? On the count of three, all those for Peggy can move to that half of the studio and those for Adam can cross over.'

The audience howled him down. 'We want love, not war,' some wit called out and they all cheered.

Ross sat down and appealed to Peggy and Adam. 'You heard them. Love, not war. Now, what do you have planned for this date, Adam?'

'That's up to Peggy. We'll do whatever she wants.' He grinned across at her. 'That's the least I can do to make up for her disappointment over the stereo.'

Ross Elliot turned to her with a roll of the eyes. 'And what do you want, Peggy?'

'Well, I might as well indulge myself while I've got the chance. At least a four-course meal, the very best wine, and it would be lovely to dance with a man who really knows how.' She raised her eyebrows at Adam. 'You do know how, don't you, or you wouldn't be starring in a musical?'

'I'll dance you off your feet,' he promised wickedly.

Ross Elliot heaved a sigh and put on a cheerful smile. 'Well, we've at least got the date settled. Tell me, Adam, does your blind date in the musical follow this pattern?'

'No. It's love at first sight between Billy Prince and Cindy Jones.'

'As opposed to war at first sight.'

Adam laughed and shook his head. 'I hope that everyone who goes to see *Blind Date* will find it as exhilarating and unforgettable as I'm sure a date with Peggy is going to be for me. In fact I don't think I can wait until tonight.' He looked across at her in twinkling enquiry. 'Let's leave them all to it and go and have some lunch.'

Unaccountably her heart leapt at the suggestion. And she was hungry! But she only had a couple of dollars in her handbag. 'Are you paying for it?' she asked hopefully.

'Naturally. There's no rule which says this date can't spread over two meals, is there?'

'No, I don't think so.'

'Well?'

'I'm starving.'

'So am I.'

He rose to his feet and Peggy eagerly followed

suit, only too pleased to have the public performance over. Not that it had been at all nerve-racking once she had met Adam Gale. His good humour had made it quite entertaining. But she had had enough. And it had been a long time since breakfast.

Ross Elliot rose to give them his dubious blessing. 'As you've seen for yourselves, I have no control over these two. I can only wish them well on their blind date. Victor says that the stars are propitious, so if anything comes of it, remember you saw them meet on this show. Peggy Dean and Adam Gale . . .'

Loud applause and a host of good wishes followed them as Adam took Peggy's hand and led her from the set. As he shut the door on the noise behind them he breathed a heavy sigh. Peggy darted an enquiring look at him. His eyes smiled down at her.

'That went very well. I like your style, Peggy Dean.'

'Yours has improved upon acquaintance,' she retorted lightly. 'I damned near died when you chose me.'

'A matter of self-preservation. The other two would've eaten me for dinner.'

'It must be sickening to be so sexy,' Peggy mocked.

'You ought to know.'

She opened her mouth, then decided it might be wiser not to continue on that tack. 'I have to collect my coat and handbag from the waiting-room.'

His eyes teased her for the evasion but he drew her arm through his and accepted the side-step. 'Lead on. The sooner we get out of here, the better.

I've had a stomachful of the publicity game.'

'You consented to it,' she reminded him pointedly.

'Another night, another woman. What's the difference?' he muttered cynically.

Peggy snatched her arm out of his loose hold and came to an abrupt halt. So he was of that ilk, was he? All cats look alike in the dark. Well, not Peggy Dean, thank you very much. Her eyes glared hostility at the all-too-handsome face.

'I've changed my mind. I don't want lunch with you. Or dinner, or anything else. I hereby renounce my prize. You're free of any obligation to me whatsoever. You can go to hell, Adam Gale!'

The image of his stunned expression gave her savage satisfaction as she marched towards the waiting-room, but she was caught and spun around before she reached the door.

'Just who the hell do you think you are?' Adam Gale snarled, his face a study of wounded pride.

'I'm the woman with a difference,' Peggy snapped back, thoroughly incensed by the restraint he was placing on her. 'Please take your hands off me.'

'I know where I'd like to lay a hand. You are completely unreasonable, did you know that?' he grated out angrily.

The gall of the man! The beastly chauvinism! Peggy wrenched one arm out of his punishing grip and slapped him.

The unexpected blow freed her completely and she whirled away in furious indignation, slamming the waiting-room door behind her and leaning against it, more because she suddenly felt very shaky than to prevent any pursuit. It was most unlikely that Adam Gale would pursue her after that little fracas.

Damn him! Never in her life had Peggy lost her temper to the extent of slapping anyone and she was appalled at herself for having done so. The insult to her sex had riled her, but it had been more than anger which had driven her to strike out.

Up until that point she had liked him. She had felt a rapport with him that she had never experienced with any other man. She had even stopped caring about the stereo-set—Adam Gale's company had become more desirable.

Fool, fool, fool, to have been taken in by a handsome face and a glib tongue! To Adam Gale she was just another female, a bit of light entertainment who presented no hassles. How could she have let herself be so affected by him? It was not like her. Not like her at all. Her hands were shaking.

She pushed herself away from the door and walked over to the drinks table. Peggy was not much of a drinker. Alcohol was expensive. Occasionally she had a glass of sherry with her parents and when her gaze found a sherry bottle she poured herself a small measure. Her nerves were jumping all over the place.

She remembered Marilyn's excuse for the vodka and for the first time, felt some sympathy for the girl. Damn Adam Gale! He should have chosen Marilyn. The sexy blonde probably wouldn't have minded being the latest in the long line of indistinguishable women who had peopled Adam Gale's life. But Peggy minded. Fiercely.

The door behind her opened. She jerked around. Defiant pride tilted her chin and flared from her eyes as she met the unsmiling gaze of Adam Gale. Well, she had wiped out that insidious laughter, she thought triumphantly. But it was a hollow triumph. There was a heavy drag on her heart which made her feel sick. Why couldn't he have gone away and left her alone? She wanted nothing more to do with a man like him.

CHAPTER FOUR

'DOES the slap cancel out the offence?' he asked ruefully.

The soft tone disarmed Peggy for a moment, the words even more so until she realised they didn't constitute any change in attitude.

'No. No, it doesn't,' she replied with uncompromising pride. 'But I *am* sorry for hitting you. You shouldn't have grabbed me. I strongly object to physical force and I'm ashamed of reacting to it on the same level. I do beg your pardon.'

'That was my line,' he said with dry irony.

She almost smiled before her mind aborted the response. What was it Victor Renshaw had said? Natural empathy . . . quick, effortless communication. But however attractive Peggy found Adam Gale, she was not about to let herself be charmed by a man who held women in contempt.

'What are you begging my pardon for? The insult or the bruises?' she asked sceptically.

He frowned. 'Did I bruise you?'

Peggy sighed and put down the glass of sherry; she did not need it after all. She felt very flat now, not the least bit jumpy. She sent Adam Gale a wry look as she stepped over to the armchair where she had left her coat and bag. 'I guess my ego is bruised more than anything, but don't let it worry you. I'll survive without your high regard.'

He made no reply and his silence depressed her as she slid one arm into her coat-sleeve. He moved so swiftly she was startled when he took up the slack of her coat, holding it for her to slide the other arm in.

'Thank you,' she muttered, completely discomposed by a sudden rush of blood to her face. What on earth was the matter with her, reacting to a normal courtesy with a blush . . . and a squeamish feeling in the pit of her stomach? She was absurdly aware of Adam Gale's physical closeness. It had to be embarrassment from having slapped him, but did embarrassment make the skin on the back of one's neck prickle?

'Peggy, will you please accept my apology for that very crass comment?'

The soft murmur caressed her ears, seducing her into a receptivity which would have given him anything he asked. Peggy was shocked at herself, so shocked she held her breath and counted quickly to ten. So he had a sexy voice. A sexy body. Sexy everything. Was she going to give up her principles and be dishonest just because Adam Gale had a personal magnetism which attracted her? She took a firm grip on herself and swung around to face him.

Damn! Did he have to be so handsome? It was extraordinarily difficult to make negative noises when those stunning blue eyes were beaming positive messages at her. She took a deep breath, stiffened her spine and blanked her own eyes to a steady neutral.

'I'll accept that you're sorry for saying what you did, but you wouldn't have said it if it wasn't the truth. That is how you feel about women, isn't it?

Just a continuing series of female faces that make
no individual impression.'

His lips curved attractively as he rubbed at the
cheek she had slapped. 'You do. One could say a
strikingly individual impression. That's all they
are.'

A smile tugged at Peggy's mouth. 'Well, maybe
you'd be less blind if you had a slap laid on you more
often.'

'I'd still like you to have lunch with me,' he
invited with a touch of whimsy that Peggy found
irresistible.

She sighed and gave in. 'Why not? I'm still
hungry.'

And a free lunch was a free lunch, Peggy argued
to herself as she let Adam Gale lead her out of the
television studio. She was not really compromising
any principles by eating with him. Provided that he
treated her with due respect, it was unfair of her to
judge him on previous relationships. A man in
Adam Gale's profession probably attracted a surfeit
of Marilyn Merrills, all keen to share his bed.

And from all Peggy had heard and observed, the
male sexual drive did not seem to be very
discriminating. She knew that Gavin had slept with
a number of girls and had not professed to love any
of them. Since she was friendly with Gavin, there
was no reason for her not to be friendly with Adam
Gale.

Except it was not quite the same. Gavin did not
make her blood tingle in the rather nerve-shaking
way it was tingling now, especially along the arm
Adam Gale was holding. Peggy did not like the

feeling that she was no longer in full control of herself just because a man was sexy. These physical reactions she was having were quite absurd.

'Why the frown?' Adam asked as he let her go to fish in his pocket for keys. They had come to a halt next to the passenger door of a huge, four-wheel-drive Range Rover. Before Peggy could think of an evasive answer Adam's mouth curved into a mocking smile. 'I suppose you had me taped with a custom-made sports model.'

She arched an eyebrow at him. 'I hate to prick your ego, but I haven't thought about you to the extent of picturing you driving anything.'

He threw back his head in a guffaw of laughter. 'Oh, I walked right into that one,' he chuckled, his eyes dancing at her with the same inner amusement he had shown during the interview. 'I really am nothing and no one to you, aren't I?'

'I wouldn't say that. You're a good singer,' Peggy blithely declared.

'Thank you,' he grinned, and having opened the passenger-door, he took her elbow to give her a lift up.

It was quite a step from the ground and Peggy was glad she was not wearing a tight skirt as she heaved herself up into the seat. Conscious of a lack of grace she kept talking to show she was not at all bothered by anything. 'It's just that I've never seen the point in fantasising over pop-stars and such-like. You shouldn't take it personally.'

Having settled herself comfortably she glanced

up into a face which was disconcertingly close to
hers. Adam Gale had stepped forward to unhook
the seat-belt for her.

'I wouldn't imagine you've ever had the need. A
girl like you could attract as many real men as she
liked,' he drawled as he stretched the belt across her
and clicked it into place. Then, instead of with-
drawing he looked straight into her eyes and smiled.
'And now that I've got you pinned down, I have this
irresistible urge to make myself real to you.'

And he kissed her. Peggy was taken by surprise
and once his mouth was on hers, curiosity stifled
any protest she might have made. On the whole,
Peggy had never found kissing all that it was
cracked up to be, but no other man had made her
blood tingle and she wondered if Adam Gale had
some other physical magic up his sleeve.

Her head was pressed back against the firm
cushioning of the seat and a hand held her face so
that he could explore her lips at will, and it was an
extremely sensuous exploration, nothing the least
bit hurried or demanding about it, but unbelievably
tantalising. So tantalising that without any conscious decision at all, Peggy opened her mouth,
inviting his invasion, and that too was incredibly
pleasant. More than pleasant—sensational enough
to seduce her out of passivity and into a response
which started as exploratory but quickly acceler-
ated into heart-thumping excitement.

It was Adam who ended it and he teased her
sensitised lips with a light finger as his eyes smiled
satisfaction into the slightly dazed darkness of hers.
'More real now?' he murmured.

It was the smug note which snapped Peggy's mind back to its usual sharpness. 'When you invited me to lunch, you didn't say I was it. I don't really find sex an adequate substitute for food,' she said flippantly.

He grinned. 'Neither do I. But it's a great appetiser.' And still grinning he closed her door, strode around the bonnet and took his place behind the driver's wheel. 'Do you like fish? There's a little place not far from here which specialises in fresh fish for lunch. Nothing fancy, but cooked to perfection.'

'Sounds fine to me,' Peggy replied airily, hoping that none of her inner perturbation showed.

She watched Adam covertly as he backed the Range Rover out of its parking slot and man-oeuvred it out on to the highway. There was no denying that she was powerfully attracted to him and he certainly knew how to kiss a girl. But then he was older and undoubtedly more experienced than any of her former would-be lovers. Whatever it was she was feeling towards him, it was undoubtedly a new experience for her. Which meant a little caution would not go astray.

'I think I should warn you that if you're thinking of me as the sweets course, you're going to be left hungry,' she stated as a matter of pride.

Adam raised a provocative eyebrow. 'Please feel free to correct me if I'm wrong, but I got the distinct impression that you enjoyed my ... uh ... initiative.'

'Oh, I enjoyed it,' Peggy admitted frankly. 'I've never been kissed with such knowing expertise. A very interesting experience. But once was enough, thank you. I really prefer kisses to have some affection behind them.'

He flashed her a smile, an absolute dazzler of a smile. 'I feel very affectionate towards you.'

Peggy's heart performed a silly little somersault and, in panicky defence, she wrenched her gaze from him and stared straight ahead. 'Do you flirt with every woman you meet?' she asked bluntly, determined to put Adam Gale's manner towards her in its proper perspective.

'Do you flirt with every man?' he retorted lightly.

She cast him a look of disdain. 'I don't flirt at all.'

'Neither do I,' he declared, and swung the Range Rover into a side-street which gave entrance to a car-park. Having brought the vehicle to a neat halt, he turned to Peggy with a devilish grin. 'And I'm finding you a very interesting experience too.'

He gave her no time for a come-back on that comment. He was out of the cabin and locking his door, the blue eyes dancing at her through the window, mockingly triumphant that he had had the last word. A burst of adrenalin pumped Peggy into instant reaction. The seat-belt was flung aside, the door catapulted open and she had leapt to the ground before Adam could lay one hand on her.

'In a hurry?' he laughed at her as he locked the door.

'My appetite doesn't need any more teasing, thank you,' she replied tartly. 'I could eat a horse right now.'

'Fish,' he corrected her with a grin which did odd things to her stomach.

'Sea-horse, then,' she muttered, wondering if it was hunger making her feel so light-headed and queasy.

Adam led her through the back entrance of a bottle-shop. Having purchased a bottle of Riesling he then walked Peggy out to the pavement of the main thoroughfare and down a couple of doors to the most unpretentious restaurant Peggy had ever seen.

Not one cent had been spent on improving the décor, if it could be called décor. The shop was exactly as it had been fitted out as a milk-bar before Peggy had been born: hard-backed booths, tacky laminex tables and battered linoleum on the floor. Yet even though it was almost two o'clock, all of the booths were occupied. Two little tables were crammed into a space near the doors to the kitchen and a man behind the counter waved Adam towards these.

'Sorry, mate. You didn't ring.'

'Doesn't matter, Harry. So long as we can eat.' He handed the bottle to the man. 'What do you recommend?'

'Schnapper's good,' was the brusque, almost indifferent reply. The bottle was uncorked and handed back, along with two cheap wine-glasses.

'Thanks. We'll have the schnapper then.'

'Right you are,' the man nodded and ambled behind them to one of the tables before passing straight into the kitchen, leaving Adam to the nicety of seeing Peggy seated.

Peggy sat down, trying to contain her amazement that Adam Gale should not only bring her to such a place, but obviously ate here quite regularly, or at least regularly enough to know the name of the proprieter, or the cook, or whatever Harry was.

Adam read her expression with considerable amusement as he took the chair opposite her. 'Not exactly the Ritz?'

She rolled her eyes around. Even the ghastly salmon-pink paint was peeling from the walls in places. Her gaze dropped to the booth closest to them and two very familiar faces caught her attention. The top-rating television newsreader and sportscaster were calmly chatting over their lunch and looking very much at home in this unlikely habitat. Peggy shook her head in stunned disbelief.

'Lots of television personalities come here for lunch,' Adam explained. 'It's close to the studios, it's good food, and Harry regards all customers as nothing more than consumers. I swear he'd call the Queen of England "mate". And she'd be smartly put down if she demanded special service. This is Harry's place and you pay to eat his fare and that's that.'

The pleasure in his voice prompted Peggy's question. 'You like to be just "mate"?'

The blue eyes stabbed her sharply. 'What do you think?' And she knew. She knew exactly why Adam Gale had chosen her instead of Marilyn and Amy, why he had overlooked her slap and persisted with his invitation for lunch, why he liked coming here to Harry's restaurant. It was because his celebrity status carried no weight with them.

Peggy had never given much thought to the personal lives of celebrities, making the obvious assumption that everything was so easy for them. Doors were opened. Everyone made way for them. People ran to be of service. But perhaps the 'star' attention did eventually pall, since it carried the unspoken demand that the star respond in a star-like way. Peggy realised it was a far more comfortable situation where nothing was expected of you.

'Do you regret becoming a pop-star?' she asked curiously.

He shrugged. 'Regrets are a waste of time. I am what I am. It has rewards as well as drawbacks,' he added carelessly.

'What do you enjoy most?'

His eyes mocked her for a moment until he realised the question had been asked out of serious interest. 'Creating music,' he replied, and there was a slight edge to his tone which implied that he did not expect to be believed.

'Not performing?'

His mouth curved into a sardonic little smile. 'All that adulation coming at me in waves over the footlights . . . mmm?'

'If you didn't like it, why did you give concerts?' Peggy countered matter-of-factly.

'It was the most effective means of communication. Isn't that your field of study . . . communication?'

It surprised her that he had remembered. And of course he was right. A performance sold his music far more effectively than a mere recording. Concerts, videos, films—they had far more impact than sound alone.

Harry emerged from the kitchen and slapped a
basket of bread-rolls and a wooden bowl of tossed
salad onto the table. 'Five minutes,' he announced,
and was off again, not waiting for a response, and
obviously not expecting one either.

Adam poured the wine into the glasses, his eyes
once more registering amusement at Peggy's startled reaction to Harry's abrupt manner. 'He means
it. Five minutes. He's giving you time to get your
bread-roll buttered, if you want one. They're fresh
from the bakery around the corner.'

Peggy took one and broke it open, noting with
pleasurable anticipation the crispy crust and the
soft warmth within. Adam passed her the butter-
dish which contained a rough slab. No fancy curls
about this restaurant! She made a private bet that
the sugar-bowl did not contain cubes either. Having
taken a slice of butter she passed the dish to Adam
who was making a mess of his roll, virtually
spraying the table with bits of crust.

'I love these. Nothing like bread-rolls fresh from
the bakery,' he remarked with relish.

'Except possibly fresh fish,' Peggy teased.

'That too,' he agreed before glancing up and
catching her wide grin. 'I am human, you know.'

The droll aside made Peggy laugh. 'I'm beginning
to believe it.'

Adam lifted his glass and sipped the wine, his
eyes glinting devilment at her over the rim. 'I'll be
happy to provide you with as much evidence as you
want,' he drawled provocatively.

Peggy lifted her own glass in a calm denial of the
havoc he was playing on her pulse. 'Oh, I can see

you're a man of many appetites, Adam,' she said
drily. 'But I tend to be very selective in my wants. A
girl in my position counts the cost of everything'

'Did you count the cost before you threw away
your prize?'

She shrugged. 'I prefer to live my life on my own
terms, and I hadn't counted on a night out with you
anyway.'

'We'll go shopping for a stereo-set after lunch.'

Peggy frowned. Much as she wanted a stereo-set,
pride insisted that she could not allow Adam Gale
to buy one for her, even though the money spent
would mean little to him. On the other hand, she did
not want to part company from him until she had to.
The effect he was having on her was so curious that
she wanted to explore it further. He was so different
to any other male of her acquaintance—challenging. Exciting. Fascinating.

'Peggy . . .'

She glanced up into determined blue eyes.

'I owe it to you. You've relieved me of the
obligation to take you out on the town. Which I'll
admit I don't enjoy, since I'm invariably pestered
by autograph-hunters and the like. I feel honour-
bound to see that you get the prize you expected to
win, particularly since I deliberately deprived you
of it.'

It was a reasonable argument and Peggy grateful-
ly accepted it. Pride agreed that she would have
won the set except for Adam's perversity in
choosing her as his date. 'That seems fair,' she
nodded.

His smile was rich with satisfaction, so much so

that Peggy squirmed inside, wondering if she should not have bent to his will. Did he think her acceptance put her under some obligation to him? Well, if he did think that, she would soon tell him otherwise.

She dismissed the uncomfortable speculation as Harry reappeared with their lunch. The aroma of steaming fish in lemon-butter sauce commanded her full attention. The plate set down in front of her contained a whole schnapper with no trimmings or accompaniments. Another plate piled high with crisply cooked chips was placed between her and Adam, and two empty plates were put next to the salad bowl for use at their convenience.

Peggy directed a bright smile at Harry's poker-face. 'Thank you.'

Surprisingly he grinned at her. 'You'll enjoy it.'

'The power of a beautiful woman,' Adam drily remarked as soon as Harry had gone. 'One smile and even Harry's face cracks open.'

Peggy shot him an irritated look. 'I was just being polite. I don't trade on sex appeal, so don't judge me by yourself, Adam Gale.'

'Everyone trades on sex appeal, either conscious-ly or subconsciously,' he mocked. 'You didn't expect me to slap you back. And you know why? Because you're a woman, and as a woman you expect to get away with hitting a man.'

Peggy had no ready answer to that, so she ignored the point and attacked the fish. It was delicious, literally melting in the mouth. Honesty forced her to admit there was truth in Adam's words but to her mind, there was still a big difference between consciously exploiting one's sex appeal as he did, and subconsciously reacting like a woman as she had. Having picked the fish clean to the bones on one side, she very carefully levered it over, stripped the skin back and coated the tender flesh with the sauce.

'As good as I promised?' Adam enquired.

'Mmh . . . perfect! How's yours?'

'The same. Help yourself to chips.'

'I will when I'm ready for them.'

'Not dieting?'

'I've got a high-burn metabolism. Besides, if I eat a big lunch I won't need much for dinner. Helps my budget.'

Peggy tucked into her meal again and had almost finished the fish when Adam made a quizzical comment.

'You know, that outfit you're wearing doesn't exactly fit the image of a poverty-stricken student.'

'The coat was a gift from my parents three years ago. The shoes I bought at Paddy's Markets. The skirt and blouse I made myself.' She flashed him a smug grin. 'I m very good at sewing. This is my one dressy outfit, and I'm glad you think it looks good, because I wanted my parents to feel proud of me. They always watch the Ross Elliot Show.'

'You don't live with them?'

'No. They live at Wyong on the Central Coast. I've got a bedsitter at Neutral Bay.'

'Alone?'

'Uh-huh.'

'Wouldn't it be more economical to share the rent with someone?'

She put her knife and fork down and picked up a few chips to nibble as she considered Adam Gale. His expression was speculative, and she was getting the impression that he was sceptical about the paucity of her finances. Although she could not think why. She shrugged off the thought and gave him a straight answer.

'I'm the only child of elderly parents. They're now pensioners and don't have much in the way of spare cash. I get the government allowance for a student living away from home, and that covers my rent. I work as a waitress on Sundays and that pays for my living costs. I prefer to do that than share my living quarters, I like having my own space. Guess it comes from being an only child. Satisfied?'

He smiled. 'A very independent lady.'

'I'm also good at competitions. I've won half the things I own.'

His smile became a grin. 'Also a smart lady.'

'And I don't drool over pop-stars,' she added for good measure.

He laughed, and he looked so devastatingly attractive that Peggy shoved some more chips in her mouth to prevent any possible drooling. 'So how about giving me a run-down on your life?' she demanded off-handedly.

'Don't you know it all?' he said with a dry touch of irony.

She glanced up into eyes which had hardened with cynicism. An odd little twinge of guilt made her realise she had prejudged this man on gossip-journalism without actually knowing any of the forces which had shaped his life. 'Do you have any family?' she asked bluntly.

The question surprised him and he did not answer immediately. He munched a handful of chips while Peggy watched him curiously, wondering why his face had suddenly been wiped of all expression.

'My father is an eminent surgeon. I have two older brothers, also in the medical profession. They all live in Melbourne. My mother deserted our very respectable household when I was two, and ran off with a musician. Needless to say, my father didn't look kindly upon my choice of career and when I threw up the education he'd planned for me, I was very much on my own. So I do know what it's like not to be able to buy what I want.'

The wry twist in the last words was the only inflexion in what had been a flat recitation of facts. Peggy's vivid imagination coloured in what had been left unsaid: the fight to forge his own destiny, the rebellion and rejection, the need to prove himself, the will to succeed.

'Has your success brought a reconciliation with your father?' she asked softly, aware that she might be treading on sensitive ground.

Adam smiled but it was a sour smile. 'I'll never be a success in my father's eyes. Giving people the transient pleasure of music is a trivial accomplishment. Cutting them up and sewing them back together is the stuff of life. And death,' he added sardonically.

Perhaps true, Peggy thought, yet the name of Adam Gale meant more to the vast majority of people than that of the world's most gifted surgeons.

People needed entertainers to relieve the boredom of daily routines. Movies, television shows, concerts ... concerts ... it was not waves of adulation that Adam Gale had wanted ... no ... but waves of approval would have been pleasant balm to wounded pride.

'I'm sorry. His judgement must be hurtful,' she said in quick sympathy.

Adam waved a dismissive hand and picked up a few more chips as he eyed her consideringly. 'No, not any more. As I said before, I am what I am, and neither my father's opinion, nor yours, nor anyone else's, really matters a damn. I like doing what I'm doing.'

'This new musical ... it means a lot to you?'

He grinned, a wide open friendly grin. 'So much that I'd probably sell my soul to promote it. And that, Peggy, is why we met today.'

'Well, you don't have to sell your soul for me. A stereo-set will do just fine,' she said cheerfully, her spirits soaring under his twinkling gaze. She helped herself to salad, a little self-conscious of her strong response to him. 'You've made me curious to hear the rest of the songs in *Blind Date*. Is there a cassette on sale?'

'It comes out next week.'

'I'll have to save up and buy it.'

'I could play you the tape this afternoon if you like. I have one in the Rover.'

Peggy's eyes sparkled with enthusiasm. 'That'd be great! I love Jenny Ross's music.'

Adam burst into laughter and Peggy flushed as she recognised her tactless gaffe. 'I like your music too,' she added forcefully.

'I'll tell Jenny . . . what an ardent . . . fan she has,' he spluttered then sucked in a deep breath. 'And Peggy, I'm not offended. I love Jenny's music too. It's been the most enlightening experience of my life, working with her.'

'Will you tell me about it?' Peggy asked eagerly. 'I mean working with Jenny Ross and composing all the songs. It'd make the tape so much more fascinating, hearing about the background.'

His smile teased her. 'That could take several hours. You might even end up spending the evening with me.'

She looked him straight in the eye and gave the answer which her inner elation insisted upon. 'I'd like that very much.'

He stared at her quizzically for a long moment before saying very slowly, 'So, I think, would I.'

Peggy had the weirdest sensation of drowning in those blue eyes, as if they were drawing her into an intimacy where she was no longer herself, but inextricably part of him. And the sense of losing herself was so real it shook the foundations on which she had built her life of independence. Everything paled into insignificance beside the desire to be with this man and share whatever he was willing to share with her.

CHAPTER FIVE

WELL, it was done now, and there was no point in fretting over it. She had protested and it was not her fault that Adam had ignored her protests. All the same, Peggy could not feel right about accepting such lavish generosity. It was all very well for Adam to insist that he was not going to play his tape on inferior machinery, but the stereo-set now residing in the back of the Range Rover was a far more expensive model than the one presented to Marilyn and Amy on the Ross Elliot Show. Peggy heaved a sigh, trying to rid herself of the weight on her conscience.

'Happy now?' Adam flashed her the smile which was increasingly reducing her backbone to jelly.

'Yes, thank you.' No point in nagging about it either. She smiled, back at him, looking forward to the hours they would be spending together, listening to music, talking. Peggy wanted to know all there was to know about Adam Gale. She felt herself more and more drawn to him with every minute she spent in his company.

As he drove them to Neutral Bay Adam described his own extensive hi-fi equipment and the various instruments he could play; piano and drums, as well as guitar, but his electronic keyboard was most favoured because of the orchestral effects he could create on it. Music seemed to completely dominate his life.

'Do you play any sport, Adam?' she asked, very aware of his tautly muscled body.

'Not any competitive sports. The odd social game of squash, and I swim in summer. Dancing . . . the kind of dancing one does in a musical . . . is a rigorous enough exercise to keep me fit.'

'I always wanted to learn dancing,' Peggy mused, rueing the lack of opportunity. 'I went to ballet lessons when I was in primary school but they weren't really serious. Just local concert stuff. There are no dance academies in country towns.'

'You're in the city now. It's not too late to learn other forms of dance. Why not give it a go?'

'No money.'

He frowned and Peggy was annoyed at herself for having pointed up her impecunious state yet again. It had never particularly worried her before. She had always managed. But somehow Adam's extravagance over the stereo-set had made her very conscious of the financial gulf between them.

'Maybe next year when I've got a steady job,' she said quickly.

Adam darted an interested look at her. 'What does a course in communication lead to? Journalism?'

'It can, but I chose to specialise in audio-visual so it's television I'd like to get into.'

'News? Documentaries? Entertainment?'

'I don't care. Getting the message across in the most effective way. That's what I want to be part of,' she said with the relish of keen ambition.

'Yes, there's the challenge,' Adam murmured,

and the warmth in his eyes sparked a lovely glow in
Peggy's soul. He understood. He liked her ambition. He shared it. And she felt a kinship with him
that she had never in her wildest dreams believed
possible. Her physical reaction to him now made
some kind of sense: instinct racing ahead of reason.

Luckily there was a parking-space near the front
entrance of the apartment-block. The two boxes
containing the player and the speakers were quite
heavy and Adam blocked Peggy's move to take one
of them.

'I'll come back for it. Grab that bag for me.' He
nodded to a nylon airways carry-all.

'What's in it?'

'A change of clothes. You don't mind if I shed
some formality, do you?'

'Not at all.'

The blue eyes danced with wicked provocation.
'You might like to change into something more
comfortable yourself.'

'My wardrobe falls a bit short of the glamour gear
you have in mind,' she retorted drily, 'and my
bedsitter falls a long way short of a courtesan's
boudoir, so have no expectations, Adam Gale, and
you won't be disappointed.'

He grinned at her over the box. 'It's your hair. All
those little ringlets make me picture you as a
courtesan.'

A smile played on her lips as she led him upstairs.
A courtesan, indeed! And here she was a virgin. She
imagined Adam's look of incredulity if she told him
that. Somehow she doubted that virgins featured

much in the pop-world. She unlocked her door and waved him in.

'Put it on the table.'

He did so, his eyes making a quick survey of her living quarters before turning back to her with a look of approval. 'The individual touch of Peggy Dean.'

She felt ridiculously pleased. The small apartment was her home away from home, and she had put a lot of personal touches into the cheap furnishings. She held out his bag to him. 'The bedroom's just behind the wall-unit and you walk through to the bathroom. Want a cup of coffee?'

'Thanks, I would.'

Peggy busied herself in the kitchenette, absurdly conscious of Adam's undressing just behind the wall-unit. Just the thought of that strong, athletic body was enough to bring a warm flush to her cheeks. It was a relief to her when he reappeared in a very casual tracksuit, althouqh the royal blue fabric accentuated his colouring, making him look even more stunningly handsome.

'I'll take this bag down and bring up the other box. Won't be a minute.'

He was off before Peggy had made an absolute fool of herself in staring at him. She shook her head and tried her utmost to get her mind in sensible working order. Common sense urged her to change out of her best clothes now, while Adam was still away. She switched off the electric kettle and raced into her bedroom, tearing off her coat on the way. She was stepping into her jeans when she heard Adam's return.

'Peggy?'

'Be right there,' she called back, reaching hurriedly for one of the fleecy-lined sloppy-joes she usually wore at home. It was in her hands when she decided it was singularly unattractive. She shoved it back in the wardrobe and took out the yellow angora sweater her mother had knitted for her. But the loose weave was too revealing to be worn without a bra. With a vexed sigh at her uncharacteristic dithering, Peggy retrieved the bra she had just discarded.

'Uh-uh. You don't need it.'

Peggy's heart catapulted around her chest as she turned to find Adam walking towards her, an amused smile curving his mouth and a warmth in his eyes which had the perverse effect of bringing goose-bumps to her skin. Rather belatedly she brought the sweater up to cover her naked breasts, then swallowed convulsively to moisten an extraordinarily dry throat.

'I didn't come in when *you* were changing,' she said, and was mortified to hear her words sounding like a childish protest against unfair play.

'I regret that your temptation wasn't as great as mine.'

Her heart halted its wild careering as Adam closed the gap between them. It stopped altogether when he began tugging the soft wool from her clutch. 'Your breasts are far too beautiful to hide.'

'Stop it! What do you think you're doing?' she cried, her voice almost strangled with shock.

'Come on, Peggy . . .' A light mockery coated the desire which was all to obvious.

'No!' She shook her head in vehement emphasis, then stepped back as a jumble of thoughts crystallised into accusation. 'The stereo-set doesn't buy me too, Adam Gale.'

The softness fled his face and the desire in his eyes was abruptly quenched. 'The day I need to buy a woman will never dawn, Peggy Dean.' His mouth curled sardonically. 'I've been around too long to get signals wrong. Perhaps you'd better reassess that honesty you dress yourself in. I'll leave you to your stereo-set.'

His departure was so abrupt that Peggy barely had time to take in his counter-accusation before she heard the front door being opened. 'Adam! Wait!' The instinctive plea burst from her lips, and without even thinking about her state of undress she ran after him, coming to a flustered halt, the sweater still clutched to her chest as she met the contemptuous look Adam turned on her from the doorway.

'I'm sorry. I don't want you to go,' she gabbled, then desperately cast around in her mind for an acceptable explanation of her behaviour. Because Adam had not been wrong and honesty demanded that she face that truth. 'It's just . . . I'm . . . I'm not used to . . . to . . . I wasn't expecting . . .'

He closed the door and leaned against it, eyeing her embarrassment in a slightly bemused fashion. 'What game are you playing, Peggy? Tell me the rules. To me it's very straightforward—I want you and you want me.'

It shook her to hear the situation stated so baldly, even though she couldn't deny it. She did want him.

But never having been to bed with a man, she was also apprehensive about what that might mean to her. 'I've . . . I've only known you for a few hours,' she said weakly.

Adam pushed himself away from the door and Peggy could not control her nervous alarm as once again he began tugging the sweater out of her grasp. She stared up at him, hopelessly tongue-tied, her body rigid with fright.

'Relax,' he said with gentle mockery. 'You'll catch your death of cold standing around half-naked. Better put this on.'

He slid it out of her nerveless fingers and pulled it over her head. In a rush of relief Peggy quickly pushed her arms into the dolman sleeves and pulled the basque down over her hips, inadvertently opening the weave across her taut breasts.

'You were right. That's one hell of a sexy garment without a bra.' He smiled into her eyes. 'But do me a favour and leave the bra off. Weren't you going to make us coffee?'

'Yes,' she got out huskily.

There was tenderness in the soft blue gaze as he brushed light fingertips down Peggy's hot cheek. 'Then why don't you go do it while I unpack these boxes? And just to set the matter entirely straight, I don't think you're a whore, Peggy, or a promiscuous little tart who'll jump into bed with anyone. And, surprising as it might seem to you, I happen to be rather particular about who shares my bed too. But you and I . . . that's something else again. I guess I can wait until you feel comfortable about it.'

Comfortable about it! Was she ever going to feel

comfortable about it? Peggy thought wildly.

Adam stepped over to the table and began tearing open one of the boxes. 'I have my coffee black with two sugars,' he tossed over his shoulder.

'Yes. Right,' she said, mentally whipping herself into action.

Peggy tried very hard to calm her disordered pulse as she reached down mugs from the overhead cupboard and spooned out instant coffee and sugar. So, this is it, she told herself firmly. This is what you've been waiting for. You'd regret it if you turned him away. It's taken years to find just one man who really turns you on, and only God knew if there would ever be another. It was stupid to get cold feet.

She was not hung up on virginity, was she? She wanted to know, didn't she? Well, here she had a tailor-made situation which answered all her heretofore objections to a sexual relationship. Except . . .

Except what? she demanded ruthlessly of herself. Except I want more from him than a quick tumble under the blankets. I want it to mean something . . . something important to both of us. Something . . . lastingly beautiful.

Oh, lordy! Get your head out of the clouds, my girl, she berated herself as the kettle whistled her back to reality. You're nothing but a cupboard romantic! Where's your logic now? You don't really believe in romance. It's just a game which leads to the same result, a man and a woman coming together in bed. So stop dithering and accept what the Fates have sent you. You're a lucky girl.

She made the coffee and carried the mugs in to the table, which was now littered with packing materials. Adam was checking wire outlets against a diagram in the working manual.

He glanced up with a smile. 'Thanks. I think the set should go over on that little table near the sofa. If you've got some sticky tape I'll run the wires above that window and over to the bookcase where the speakers can stand at either end. That should give you the best sound in here.'

Peggy nodded. 'I'll get the sticky tape and scissors.'

'I see you like the Fauves artists,' he commented as she turned away.

She turned back, surprised that he had identified the prints on her walls.

'I prefer the Impressionists myself,' he went on, amused by her surprise. 'You'd probably like Cass Flemming's work.'

'Cass Flemming?'

'You don't look around the Sydney art galleries?

She shook her head. 'Only the New South Wales art gallery. When there's a special exhibition on.'

'Well, I don't know if Cass has made it there, but Tony has. He won the last big landscape competition. You might have seen that painting. *The Windsurfer* by Tony Knight?'

'Yes, I did. It was beautiful. Shimmering with light. You know him?'

'He and Cass designed the stage scenery for *Blind Date*. Cass did the pop-world sets . . . striking lines and vibrant with colour . . . that's her style. And

Tony's sets for the love-scenes are pure romance. Beautiful!'

Romance! Did Adam believe in romance? 'Are you a romantic at heart, Adam?' she asked bluntly.

The blue eyes flashed up at her, hard and cynical. 'Our society is so damned stuffed, we need a few dreams to make it bearable.'

She sighed and went into the kitchenette to get the tape and scissors. His answer had disappointed her and yet he was only saying what she herself had thought about entertainment only a few hours ago.

'You remind me of Cass,' Adam remarked when she returned, and there was a mischievous glint in his eye as he grinned at her.

'Oh? In what way?' Peggy was severely jolted by an uncharacteristic stab of jealousy.

'She loves cutting people down to size. Tony does too. As I've heard tell, they cut each other into pieces before they married, though you'd never guess it now. They're a great couple.'

The jealousy receded. Cass Flemming was no threat.

'Jenny Ross is married to Tony's brother, Robert,' Adam continued. 'If you're heading into the television world, you should have heard of him. Robert Knight?'

'Yes, of course. The man's a genius with musical shows.'

'He directed the last TV Special I did two years ago. I discussed the idea of *Blind Date* with him and Jenny then, and they were as keen as I was to develop it into a show.'

'So Robert Knight's the director?'

'Uh-huh.' Adam's grin was full of happy warmth. 'With me and Jenny and Tony and Cass, all putting our bit in. He gets stroppy with what he calls unwarranted interference, but Jenny only has to smile at him and he's putty in her hands. He adores her.'

'What's she like?' Peggy asked curiously. Clearly Adam was very much at home with these people. His liking for them coloured his voice and softened his eyes in a way which made her wish he had never learnt cynicism.

Adam picked up the set and carried it over to the table near the sofa. He placed the speakers on the bookshelves and gathered the wires into his hand. 'Pass me pieces of tape, will you, Peggy?'

She did so as he trailed the wires around the architrave above the window. 'Tell me about Jenny Ross,' she prompted, too interested to let him drop the subject and hoping to keep Adam in this pleasant, confidential mood.

'She's a very warm, unassuming person. She's little. Small-boned. Brown hair. Freckles. Not much to look at superficially, but she's got this remarkably expressive face which lights up like a ...' He hesitated, searching for the right word, then shrugged. 'Hard to describe, but if you'd ever seen her sing one of her songs, you'd be transfixed by the play of emotion on her face.'

'I didn't know she sang.'

'She doesn't for the public but she has a sweet voice. Perfect pitch, but without the volume to make it sell. Besides, Jenny would rather die than be a performer. She'll only sing for family or close friends.'

'But you like being a performer.'

Adam flashed her a wary look, measuring the intent behind the words. 'Yes, I like it.' He fastened the last bit of tape necessary to hold the wires in place before turning to her full face. The blue eyes were hard again. 'I'm arrogant enough to think that I can put over my music better than anyone else. Since I wrote it, I know best what it's about, and as you were kind enough to say, I'm a good singer.'

Peggy smiled. 'Not arrogance, Adam.'

He raised one eyebrow sardonically but a twinkle had crept into his eyes. 'You sure about that?'

'You're a great performer,' she declared convincingly. It was the truth.

He laughed and drew her into his arms. 'Coming from you, that's an accolade which means something.'

'There aren't many pop-stars who can make their presence felt without some gimmick or other. You're really quite electric, all by yourself,' Peggy said in a rush, all too aware of a sudden difficulty in breathing and a rapidly pounding heart.

'Electric. Is that how it feels to you?' he murmured, running one hand up into the mass of ringlets at the back of her neck. A little smile played on his lips as he added, 'I'd have to admit it's been quite a charge meeting you, Peggy Dean. Let's try that interesting experience again, mmmh?'

His lips grazed across hers in a slow, experimental manner. Peggy instantly fell under the spell of his physical magic. She was not only willing, but eager to experience the complete range of that magic. But Adam was no longer intent on forcing the pace. His hands gently moulded her body to his using a sensual pressure which denied any urgent passion, yet leaving her in no doubt that desire had been aroused by the contact he was so knowingly orchestrating.

In the back of Peggy's mind was the recognition that he was imposing his body on hers, seducing a submission to the harder strength of his masculinity. But the pleasure swimming through her veins made pliancy the only possible response. And with her unhesitant surrender to his will came a sudden deepening of his kiss, a probing of exciting intimacy which Peggy returned with uninhibited fervour.

Passion exploded between them, a hungry, voracious possession of each other. Their bodies strained closer, grinding together with a sexual urgency which their hands pushed to a feverish level.

'This can't wait,' Adam breathed harshly, already walking, blundering backwards in haste towards the bedroom.

Peggy clung to him, totally abandoning herself to the dizzying, exciting world of sensation he had led her into, intoxicated beyond caring when he dragged off her clothes and discarded his. Adam virtually tossed her on the bed and for one flicker of a moment Peggy felt a ripple of fear at the sheer aggression of his maleness as he leaned over her, but then he was with her and as the hard muscularity of his body impressed itself on her softness, everything seemed utterly right.

Driven by the blazing heat of their desire, they made excessive, frenzied demands on each other's bodies, wanting to own, to indelibly mark their ownership with the power of their need. A primitive exultation throbbed through Peggy as Adam poised to take her. She looked up at him, eyes wantonly inviting this ultimate sharing and the driven tautness of his face excited her further. Her breath caught in her throat as her inexperienced body instinctively tensed against the alien force of Adams entry; then dazedly she saw his face freeze into shock.

'No!' The word broke from his lips in a hoarse gasp.

To her total incomprehension, a blaze of hatred leapt from his eyes and in a rejection which was tearingly abrupt, he flung himself away from her, pulling up on the edge of the bed, almost doubled over, heaving in deep breaths and shaking his head from side to side.

'You bitch! Goddamned little bitch! Suckered in all the way.' The savage mutter accompanied a swoop to snatch his clothes off the floor. Then he was on his feet and dressing in swift, jerky movements, all the while directing a barrage of bitter contempt at Peggy.

'You're still intact, my clever little calculator. You can't lay the violated virgin bit on me and you can't yell rape either, so you've lost the whole bloody game. Though I'll hand it to you, Peggy Dean, you're the best tactician I've met in a long, long time. You almost deserve a pay-off for the quality of the act. But when you've been stung on the virgin play, you don't feel very generous the second time around. Find yourself some other sucker!'

His words reverberated around her brain, thudding like hammer blows to an anvil which was still muffled by the needs which had been left so jarringly unfulfilled. Little shivers were running over her skin and an aching weakness dragged at every nerve. Peggy could not summon the will or the energy to move and her mind was too dazed to form any speech at all. While he had struck out at her, again and again with vicious contempt, she had lain where he had left her, her dark eyes huge with shock, staring at him like a helpless, wounded animal.

The blue eyes were hard chips of ice, stabbing her quivering body as they moved down her length. 'You do have quality merchandise. I'll grant you that. I should've known the offer was too good to be true.' His mouth curled in self-disgust. 'I might've even paid for it if you'd been honest.' Then his gaze whipped back to hers, hard and unforgiving. 'I hope you feel as rotten as I do.'

He turned on his heel and was gone, not waiting for any form of reply. The slam of the front door punctuated his exit.

Peggy did not move. She did not move until her naked body felt chilled to the bone. Then stiffly, clumsily, she climbed under the bedclothes and tucked them around her. It was a long, long time before she could clear her mind for enough rational thought to make some logical sense of Adam's blistering tirade.

It was her virginity that had triggered it. There had been some bad experience in his past relating to a virgin he had taken to bed, and who had taken him for a lot of money. The threat of scandal? Blackmail? Impossible to guess all the facts but whatever had happened had scarred Adam Gale, and was a telling factor in his deep cynicism where women were concerned.

But why had Adam made such monstrous accusations against her? So she had not told him she was a virgin. In the wild heat of passion it simply had not occurred to her to tell him. There was a first time for everyone, wasn't there? Were you supposed to make a song and dance about it? Surely a man of any sensitivity would simply accept it as evidence of the strength of her feeling for him ... something that no other man had drawn from her. A wave of black depression rolled over Peggy, adding its weight to the malaise which had possessed her body since Adam had left it.

Why had he assumed she would sell herself for money? Hadn't she made her attitude clear on that point? Perhaps too clear. Too emphatic. The lady doth protest too much? She had talked too much about money and her lack of it, and Adam had worn an air of reserve whenever she had spoken of her circumstances.

Virginity ... given up without a word ... and no money. Innocence—corruption. This, then was the equation from the past which had injected its poison, bringing a convulsive reaction which had made Adam lash out with such destructive force that the relationship which had seemed to promise so much was now finished.

Tears trickled from the corners of Peggy's eyes and were fed by a relentless well of desolation. She did not fight it. She felt too weak and sick to fight anything. She turned her head into the pillow and silently cried herself to sleep.

CHAPTER SIX

PEGGY breathed a cautious sigh of relief as the lecture on Social History began. She adopted an air of listening. A Biro was poised in her fingers, ready to make notes if anything of importance struck her ears, but her mind was taking a much-needed rest.

It seemed that everyone in the Institute had watched yesterday's Ross Elliot Show. At least everyone in her faculty. Dear Gavin had seen to that. And of course the lunch-time slot of the show had been ideal for gaining a large viewing audience. They had all been riotously amused by Peggy's performance and were now avidly curious about her 'blind date' with Adam Gale.

Questions had been tossed at her all morning but the main barrage had come over lunch in the cafeteria. She hoped that her flippant replies had projected the nonchalance she was far from feeling. A lot of the curiosity had dimmed and the sly innuendoes had fallen flat on her revelation that she had traded the date for a stereo-set.

But Gavin had kept watching her. Damn his eyes! All the same, she was reasonably sure that her composure had not slipped under the pressure he had directed at her. Surely everyone was now convinced that there had been nothing at all between her and Adam Gale. She wanted the subject closed. Finished. Just as finished as their brief relationship.

The lecture droned on and was followed by another, the last of the day. Peggy forced herself to stay on afterwards and sit over a cup of coffee with the usual crowd. She defused the last little shots of speculation with studied boredom, agreed to a game of squash the following day, declined to make up a four for table-tennis on the excuse of having washing to do, then took herself home.

She did do some washing. And ironing. And every other household chore she could think of. The stereo-set kept staring her in the face, building up an insane desire to get an axe and chop it into a thousand pieces. But sanity prevailed, and the set remained intact and unplayed. Adam had left his tape of *Blind Date* on the table. Peggy had shoved it in the bookcase, out of sight and unplayed. If she had known where to send it she would have posted it to him. As it was, not even the lure of Jenny Ross's music could break Peggy's resolve to have nothing to do with anything belonging to Adam Gale.

Pride could not salve the hurt she was feeling but it helped keep it within manageable boundaries. She told herself that Adam Gale was part of a fantasy-world and she had deluded herself into thinking they had shared something special. The bubble of magic had burst at the best possible time, before she had really thrown herself in at the deep end. She could have been hurt far more than she had. She was lucky he had cut her out of his life, even though the surgery had been cruel. She had her own life to live, and thank God she wasn't as twisted up in her mind as he obviously was!

In the days that followed Peggy kept herself very busy. The curiosity about Adam Gale was soon dropped at the Institute and life continued as before. They were given a new assignment on interpersonal communication and Peggy readily agreed to Gavin's suggestion that they get together on it and see if they could produce something spectacularly original.

'When?' she asked, as practical as ever.

He shrugged. 'How about I come home with you now? I've got nothing on tonight. Have you?'

Nothing any night, she thought despondently, then quickly clamped down on such stupid maundering. 'All right, we might as well get straight into it. But, Gavin . . .' She sliced him a caustic look. 'I'm not feeding you, so go buy your own provisions for the evening.'

He eyed her speculatively for a moment before drawling, 'You know, Peggy, you've been a mite short with me ever since the Adam Gale affair.'

Peggy stared him down. 'Perhaps I didn't find all the fuss as funny as you did.'

'But it was funny, Peggy. Funny damned peculiar,' he said with sly emphasis. 'Not that I'm a devotee of astrology, but I couldn't help but agree with that old charlatan, Victor Renshaw. The sparks were flying and I'd give a lot to know what put them out. Curiouser and curiouser, as the March Hare said. Or was it Alice herself?'

'You're living in Wonderland, Gavin. I've never

in my life met a man so full of himself as Adam Gale. Except perhaps you,' she added with one eyebrow raised mockingly.

He grinned. 'Well, I am good. No point in false modesty.'

She gave an exaggerated sigh. 'Food, Gavin, if you're coming with me.'

'Tell you what, just to soothe any ruffled feathers, I'll even buy you a couple of pies.'

'Do that. You owe me. But not for ruffled feathers,' she added drily.

'One of these days, Peggy Dean . . .'

'Yes?' she asked with limpid innocence.

Gavin rolled his eyes at her and scooted off to the cafeteria. Peggy felt quite proud of herself as she walked out to the bus-stop. She had fended off Gavin's probe without too much heartburn. Surely it was only a matter of time before she could dismiss the whole disturbing encounter with Adam Gale as a dream. A bad dream.

Gavin joined her just as the bus for Circular Quay pulled in. There were no seats to be had together but Peggy was more than content to sit alone. She hoped Gavin's fertile mind would find another subject to gnaw on before they caught the ferry across the harbour.

It was cold and windy, but despite the discomfort of the weather Peggy always enjoyed the ferry-ride to Neutral Bay. It was full of interest and beauty, no matter how bleak the day. Gavin was none too pleased when she insisted on staying outside on the deck.

'You're a nature nut,' he grumbled. 'Must come

from having been brought up in the country. Unhealthy, you know.'

She laughed at him as he dug his hands into the pockets of his windcheater and hunched his shoulders over. 'You shouldn't spend so much time in bedrooms. There's more to life than sex,' she declared.

'How would you know?' he scoffed.

She flashed him a derisive look. 'Give it a rest. What do you think of a political scenario for our assignment?'

He argued pros and cons until they were ensconced at the table in her bedsitter, and then they began developing a theme from the ideas they could agree upon. They had only been at it for an hour or so when Gavin declared he was hungry. Peggy put the pies in the oven and decided she would cook a batch of chips to go with them.

'Not a bad-looking stereo-set,' Gavin remarked and got up to examine it. 'Good sound?'

'Yes,' Peggy answered briefly. It had sounded good in the shop—she had not yet felt inclined to play anything on it at home. Of course that was only a matter of time too. It was hers, she had earned it fair and square, and she would use it. Eventually. Nevertheless she felt relieved when Gavin moved away from it and pottered through the shelves of her bookcase.

She was in the act of turning the chips over in the fry pan when a fanfare of trumpets blared across the room, completely shattering her peace of mind. She knew exactly what tape it was even though she had never heard it. 'Turn it off!' she shrilled.

A clash of cymbals drowned out her voice. Peggy
dropped the fork and rushed into the living-room,
her heart thumping like one of the drums which was
beating in the *Blind Date* theme.

'Turn it off!'

Even she heard the note of hysteria in her voice
and a flood of self-conscious colour scorched into
her cheeks as Gavin raised his eyebrows at her.

'What's the problem? Sounds interesting.'

'Just turn it off, Gavin. Now!' she bit out
vehemently.

He shrugged and flicked the *Off* switch.

'Rewind it, replace the cassette in its case and
return it to the bookcase,' she commanded tersely.
Cheeks still flaring with heat, she swung on her heel
and marched back into the kitchenette, knowing
full well she had over-reacted and hating herself for
it. Damn Adam Gale! And damn his music too, she
thought fiercely.

'What's wrong with a bit of music while we eat?'
Gavin demanded, strolling into the kitchenette
after her and propping himself on her stool.

Peggy tried for carelessness but her voice came
out flat, 'It's not my tape.'

'So?'

'I don't want it played.'

'It's not going to hurt the tape. What is it
anyway?'

'What's what?'

'Don't be dense. The music.' He screwed up his
face. 'Those cymbals and drums . . . I've heard a
lead-in like that. Can't think . . .'

'Take the pies out of the oven, Gavin,' she cut in impatiently. 'These chips are cooked.'

'Any bread and butter?'

Thank God for the bottomless pit that was Gavin's stomach, Peggy though with relief. With his attention successfully diverted on to food, she could concentrate on relaxing the nerves which had been jangling ever since the first trumpet blast. It had brought the memory of Adam too close. She could almost feel his presence. And to her horror, she wanted him here with a desire so strong that she felt sick.

Gavin cleared a space at the table and they sat down to their meal. Peggy wished she had not cooked chips. They reminded her of the lunch she had shared with Adam at Harry's place. She cut up her meat pie and forced herself to eat it.

'*Blind Date*! Adam Gale's new hit. That's what it is,' Gavin stated triumphantly.

Peggy's heart plummeted. Trust Gavin's mind to keep gnawing over an unanswered question. There was only one way to neutralise his interest and that was to satisfy his curiosity one way or another. 'Actually it's the tape of the whole musical. It belongs to him and he left it here accidentally when he set up the stereo for me. I don't feel I should touch it since it's his personal possession. I'll leave it at the theatre for him when the musical opens.'

'That's tomorrow night, isn't it?'

'Yes.'

'Did you get the two free tickets?'

'No. They weren't part of the deal I made with him.'

'Funny deal,' Gavin muttered. 'Why didn't he want to go out with you?'

'Gavin, it was I who didn't want to go out with him,' she said with pointed weariness for the subject. 'You're getting to be a pain in the neck about Adam Gale. Do you think we could get back on to work?'

He heaved a sigh and pulled a grimace. 'As you like. But one of these days . . .'

They got back to work. Peggy was too unsettled to give her full concentration to it, but Gavin was only too pleased to be the dominant partner in pushing ideas. Hours went by unnoticed. Peggy was making them both yet another mug of coffee when the doorbell rang.

'I'll get it,' Gavin offered, pushing himself away from the table.

Peggy frowned at the oven clock. 'It's past eleven. Have you got someone calling for you, Gavin?'

'No such luck. Didn't even realise it was so late.'

'Put the safety-chain on before you open the door. God knows who it is at this hour.'

'Will do.'

Peggy automatically listened for the rattle of the chain being slotted into place. The click of the door-catch immediately followed, then came Gavin's amused voice. 'Well, well, what do you know?'

'Who is it?' Peggy called out, curiosity getting the better of discretion.

'Your friend, Adam Gale.'

Adam's soft baritone instantly followed Gavin's

chirpy announcement. 'I'm sorry, I didn't realise
Peggy had a visitor. I'll . . .'

Gavin blithely interjected, 'Not at all, dear chap.
I don't count as a visitor, and I'm quite sure you do.
Come on in. Peggy's just making coffee and I'll be
going away soon anyway. Gavin Howes is the
name.'

Peggy found herself clutching the edge of the
bench. The blood had drained from her face at the
first sound of Adam's voice. Questions darted
through her mind, jolting it into activity. What was
Adam doing here? At this hour? When people were
going to bed. Bed! Oh God! Did he really think . . .
Had he come to . . .

He had come in! The sound of the door closing
threw Peggy into a panic. What was she to do or
say? In front of Gavin. Cool . . . play it cool, the
voice of common sense insisted. She wheeled to face
the two men as they appeared in the kitchen
doorway.

'Another mug for Adam, Peggy,' Gavin said with
an obvious relish for the situation.

'Hello, Adam,' she said tightly. 'I didn't expect to
see you again.'

She hoped that none of her inner turmoil showed
as the blue eyes scanned her face. He was dressed in
the same tracksuit he had worn when he left her,
and although he looked tired and strained, his
physical presence tore at her heart.

'I apologise for calling so late, Peggy. I wouldn't
have rung if there hadn't been a light on, but . . . I
hope I'm not interrupting anything,' he said with
wary politeness.

'Gavin and I were working on an assignment,' she stated flatly.

'Which we've broken the back of,' Gavin declared cheerfully. 'We can put the finishing touches to it tomorrow or whenever.'

He was going to leave her with Adam if she didn't do or say something fast. 'I'd prefer to finish tonight, Gavin.' Inspiration struck. 'I'm sure Adam's only come for his tape. I'll get it.' She quickly strode past them and over to the bookcase, only to find that the cassette was not where she had placed it. 'Where is it, Gavin?'

'Oh, sorry! Didn't put it back.' He strolled over to the stereo-set, taking his time while he prattled on. 'I started playing it to test out the stereo and Peggy almost went off her brain. Exaggerated sense of integrity the girl has! Wouldn't let it be played because it was yours, Adam.' He picked up the cassette and turned, smiling. 'Wouldn't have thought you'd have minded?'

'No, I wouldn't have minded.' His gaze moved sharply to Peggy. 'Didn't you play it at all?'

'No, it wasn't mine. I don't take what belongs to other people,' she replied, each word clipped with icy precision.

'See what I mean?' Gavin commented airily. 'Got the pride of the devil, our Peggy has.'

'Our Peggy? Are you related?' Adam enquired.

'In a manner of speaking. I've been intimately acquainted with that quirky brain of hers for the last four years. One of these days . . .'

'Gavin!' Peggy bit out impatiently 'I doubt that Adam is interested in our relationship. Please give him the tape so he can go.'

'Go? Do you want to go, Adam? I would've thought you'd like to relax over a cup of coffee. Wind down. You have just come from a dress rehearsal, haven't you? Tomorrow night's the big night. I imagine everyone's a bit uptight about it. Wouldn't you like to stay a while? Get your mind off it?'

Peggy directed a look of pure venom at Gavin but he was enjoying himself hugely and no way was he going to let her or Adam off the hook if he could keep them wriggling.

'Yes, it would be pleasant,' came Adam's smooth agreement.

Peggy's eyes threw a furious challenge at him. It was on the tip of her tongue to tell both him and Gavin to get the hell out of her home, but pride suddenly crumpled under the powerful attraction of those insidious blue eyes, and the electric kettle began to whistle, breaking into the tension.

'You might as well take a seat then,' she muttered ungraciously. 'I'll make the coffee.'

'I'll move my stuff off the table,' Gavin offered, full of sweetness and light.

Peggy gritted her teeth and swept into the kitchen.

'You know, Adam, all of us . . . Peggy's friends at The Institute . . . watched that Ross Elliot Show to see how she'd go,' Gavin blathered on. 'We thought you two really hit it off. Of course we know how sharp-tongued Peggy can be . . .'

'I enjoy a quick wit,' Adam said blandly.

'Oh, so do I. Fencing with Peggy is one of the

chief pleasures of my life. Mind you, it's the only pleasure she hands out freely. I keep telling her . . .'

'Gavin!' Peggy's voice spoke murder. 'You are beginning to bore me.'

'Am I really? Well, if that's how you feel I'd better leave.'

Peggy was already on her way to the table, a mug of steaming coffee in each hand. She could hardly believe her eyes when Gavin hopped up, stuffed his things in his bag and slung it over his shoulder.

He grinned at her, sheer devilment in his eyes. 'Never let it be said I stayed where I wasn't wanted. Delighted to have met you, Adam. Don't get up. I'm off. Good night, Peggy. See you tomorrow.'

'Gavin!' she exploded as he headed for the door.

'Sorry about the coffee,' he tossed back at her. 'Throw it down the sink.'

The door was snapped firmly shut before Peggy could say another word. She stood there, breathing shallowly as her pulse-rate leapt into overdrive. Coffee slurped on to her fingers. She looked down; her hands were shaking. Adam stood up, and her eyes flared a warning as he stepped towards her.

'You come any closer and I'll throw this all over you,' she cried defiantly.

'It's spilling.'

'I'll clean it up after you've gone. I didn't ask you in, I don't want you here. Please go, and take your tape with you.'

'I don't want the tape, Peggy. That's not why I came. I needed to see you, talk to you.'

The gentleness of his speech completely unnerved her. Hot coffee was streaming down her

hands. She turned, walked back into the kitchen
and tipped the lot down the sink. Keeping her back
turned to Adam so that her resolve could not be
weakened by the force of physical attraction, she
took a deep breath and spoke as calmly as she could.

'You said quite enough last time. I can't imagine
there's any more to be said—not anything I want to
hear anyway.'

'I was wrong. I could try to explain my . . . my
behaviour, but that wouldn't excuse it. I didn't stop
to think . . .' He hesitated, then sucked in a sharp
breath before continuing. 'I was once the victim of a
vicious piece of entrapment which almost broke me
just as my career was taking off. Since then I've
been careful to associate only with women who've
obviously been around. It came as a shock when I
found you were . . . inexperienced. You hadn't
warned me or tried to stop me, and I leapt to what I
realise now was a totally unwarranted assumption.'

He paused and Peggy writhed at the memory of
her abandoned response to his lovemaking. What
had he thought of her . . . that she was a sex-hungry
wanton?

A heavy sigh ushered in his next words. 'I regret,
very much, the savage way I spoke and acted. It's
been preying on my mind ever since, and I'd be
grateful if you could bring yourself to accept my
apology.'

She whipped around, stung by the selfishness of
his speech. 'So that you'll feel better?' she demanded scathingly.

He stood in the kitchen doorway, stiffly tall,
heartbreakingly handsome, and distinctly ill at

ease. 'I wish I could make *you* feel better but I don't know how to.'

The simple sincerity of the words brought a lump to Peggy's throat, choking her into silence.

Adam lifted his hands in a gesture which was half-appeal, half-apology. 'I'd give anything to have that afternoon over again. I'm so sorry for . . . for what happened. You weren't to know that I'd had such an experience. I'd hate to think that what I've done might affect you . . . make you wary or cause you to shrink from . . . from being touched. I hope you can forget my stupidity, even if you can't forgive it.'

Still she could not speak. Her chest felt painfully constricted and tears were pricking at her eyes.

Adam sighed and drew an envelope from a side-pocket. 'I brought you a ticket for tomorrow night. I don't suppose you'll want to use it, but there it is anyway.' He dropped it on to the nearest cupboard and lifted bleak eyes to her. 'I'd like you to come. I'd like to give you some pleasure to make up for the pain I inflicted. But . . .' He heaved another sigh. 'Thank you for at least listening to me. It's more than I did with you.'

He went swiftly, before Peggy had wits enough to make any kind of decision. She was left standing in the kitchen. Slowly and carefully her mind revolved and examined everything he had said. An admission of misjudgement, an apology, a wish to make some reparation: but no suggestion, not even the remotest hint that he would like to take up a relationship with her. Guilt had driven him to this visit. He had wanted to relieve his conscience of her.

'Preying on his mind'. Had he been distracted from giving full concentration to his performance? The fact that he had called on her after his dress rehearsal seemed to point that way. Cleansing his soul before the grand première. Yes, that had probably been his motive. Nothing really to do with her at all. It was finished. A wry grimace twisted her mouth. And she had been fool enough to think he wanted her!

Her eyes fell on the envelope Adam had dropped on the cupboard. She walked over and picked it up, slit it open and extracted the ticket. Front stalls, not too close to the orchestra pit: probably the best position in the theatre to see and hear everything on stage. Such a ticket would be worth a great deal, well beyond Peggy's pocket. But she had expected to win two of these tickets on the Ross Elliott Show. In a way she was entitled to it. Had Adam thought of that? She shook her head dejectedly and wandered into the living-room. Did she want to see *Blind Date*? No, the question was—could she bear to see it? Adam had not taken the tape. It was still sitting on the table. On impulse Peggy snatched it up and inserted it into the stereo-player. She would listen to it, then she would decide what to do.

By the time one side of the cassette had played through, Peggy's emotions were so shredded, she turned the set off and went to bed. Adam's voice and the strong personality he was projecting from his songs had been torment enough, but the yearning for love, so poignantly written into Jenny

Ross's songs for Cindy Jones, had struck a chord in Peggy which throbbed so painfully that she could not have sat through any more of it. She did not sleep well. Her preparation for the day was less than energetic and her composure was far too brittle to face up to Gavin and his sly little probes. She was careful to avoid meeting him before their first morning lecture at the Institute, but he fell into step beside her as they changed rooms for the second.

'You're looking rather seedy this morning,' she commented, employing attack as defence.

'You're seeing a survivor of an all-night binge.'

'No sleep for the wicked.'

'I was performing an act of charity. Adam wanted company.'

The name hit Peggy like a blow. It took her several seconds to recover from the unexpectedness of Gavin's tack. 'Oh? How did you two get together?' she asked with the most casual air she could manage.

'I waited a few minutes for him and when he came out, I asked for a lift home. Public transport is not at its best at that hour.'

She slanted him a derisive look. 'You really do have more gall than any other ten people put together.'

'Peggy love, the man has connections. You're welcome to enjoy your fine sense of integrity, but it's a dog-eat-dog world, and yours truly is not above cultivating an influential friend, particularly one who knows all the names in television. Why don't you give the guy a chance? I like him.'

Peggy digested the question slowly, looking for

what lay behind it. Gavin could either be testing her feelings or he knew something she didn't know. 'What makes you think he wants a chance?' she tossed off carelessly.

Gavin threw her a mocking glance. 'I was there last night, remember? He didn't come to pick up a tape. I could've cut the tension between you two with a knife, and he emerged from your private little tête-à-tête looking sick. Very simple for me to deduce that he hadn't got what he wanted. Now, given that you'd knocked him back, why do you suppose he agreed to take me home and accept my hospitality?'

'The natural charm of your scintillating company?'

'Don't be thick, Peggy. It doesn't become a smart girl like you. My one attraction for Adam Gale is that I know you well—as well as anyone knows you.'

Angry colour burnt into her cheeks. 'He talked about me?'

Gavin eyed her with sharp interest, deliberately holding her in suspense as he gauged the strength of her reaction. Peggy stared coldly back at him.

'Uh-uh, not a word,' he finally admitted. 'But he listened while I told him everything I knew. And he wasn't bored at all. He did drink a lot but he wasn't bored. Now what does that tell you, Peggy?'

She sniffed. 'That you'd probably sell your mother's soul if you could see an advantage to yourself.'

Gavin arched a sceptical eyebrow at her as she settled into a chair. Peggy ignored him, making a business of getting ready to take notes. The lecturer arrived, and Gavin dropped into the chair next to her.

'None so blind as those who don't want to see,' he muttered in her ear.

The lecture began but Peggy paid little heed to it. Her mind seethed with questions. Why had Adam gone home with Gavin and got drunk? And what had Gavin told him about her . . . just plain facts, or had he indulged in his usual brand of speculation? The trouble with Gavin was that he was altogether too fond of speculating. And too damned good at it! But was he right? Could Adam's interest in her be more than a case of bad conscience?

The ticket . . . perhaps it was more than a peace-making gesture. Perhaps it represented a very real desire for her to be at the première tonight, not only to see the show but because . . . She frowned, wondering what might have been said last night if only she had not been so hostile. Gavin obviously believed that Adam did want another chance with her and Gavin was very sharp. If he was right . . . well, she was not going to cut off her nose to spite her face.

It was stupid to pretend that Adam Gale didn't mean anything to her. He did, more than she liked admitting, considering his treatment of her. But he had apologised, and the apology had sounded genuine. And he had left her the ticket. So, all right; she would go to the première of *Blind Date*. Perhaps it would lead somewhere.

A little smile tugged at Peggy's mouth. It really was ridiculous to feel so light-hearted all of a sudden. The ticket probably meant nothing but a seat in a theatre. But she could not quite smother the hope which had begun dancing a dizzy delight along her veins.

CHAPTER SEVEN

PEGGY glanced once more at her watch. Eight-o-two. She walked towards the stalls entrance, deciding it was better to be ahead of the warning bell. While it had been fascinating to watch the cream of society and the entertainment world showing off the extremes of fashion, she did not want to be caught in a crowd and risk being late to her seat.

Never having been to a première before, Peggy was not sure if the show would actually start at eight-fifteen, but she could sit and watch others being ushered to their seats. Besides, she was beginning to feel a little self-conscious in her houndstooth coat. Once shown to her seat she could take it off and tuck it behind her legs. The red blouse and black velvet skirt were not exactly *haute couture*, but the outfit could pass as evening-wear and she would not feel quite so out of place.

'Peggy!'

Gavin? She swung around and incredulity changed to startled surprise as she beheld a tidy, dinner-suited Gavin striding towards her, his familiar grin topping the unexpected elegance.

'You can close your mouth. It's me all right.'

'I'd never have believed you dressed up so well if I hadn't seen it,' she declared, hiding her discomfort at being outshone by him. 'How come you're here?'

'More to the point, Peggy love, how come you're here?'

'Adam gave me a ticket last night,' she said with forced nonchalance.

'Did he now?' The green eyes sharpened with speculation. 'He arranged one for me at the box-office. Also invited me to the party after the show, which is why I'm togged up like this. Are you partying too?'

'No.'

Gavin frowned. 'I wonder . . . where's your seat, Peggy?'

'In the stalls.'

'Mine's in the mezzanine so that can't be it. Unless . . .' He brightened. 'You play your cards too close to the chest, Peggy. Meet me here after the show and I'll take you to the party.'

'No!'

'For Chrissake! Can't you see . . .'

Two angry spots of colour burnt into her cheeks. 'You go your way and I'll go mine, Gavin. And mine is not going where I haven't been invited.'

'But . . .'

'You're not Adam Gale's mouthpiece. He can speak for himself. Good luck to you, but leave me out of it.'

She turned on her heel and marched towards the stalls entrance, head held high in a proud denial of the turbulence in her mind. Was she being stupid or was Gavin being too damned clever? What did Adam want? she asked herself distractedly as she handed her ticket to the usher. The man looked her up and down. His appraisal and the fact that even

Gavin had worn a dinner-suit made Peggy all the
more self-conscious of her clothes. The usher was
probably wondering what she was doing at such a
fashionable affair and Peggy wished she had not
come.

Her cheeks burnt all down the aisle. It was with
some dismay that she found the seats around hers
already occupied by a group of people in the most
formal of formal clothes, and they all looked at her
as she removed her coat. In a burst of belligerence
Peggy glared back at them. She had as much right
as anyone to be here, and they were being
downright rude for staring at her.

The woman in the seat next to Peggy's suddenly
smiled and her face lit up with a welcoming
warmth. 'Hello. I'm so glad you came.'

For a moment Peggy's mind boggled. Who was
this woman, and why was she speaking to her with
such an air of pleasure? 'I beg your pardon, but I'm
afraid I don't know you,' Peggy said politely and
sank into her seat, feeling decidedly awkward with
the situation.

'Didn't Adam . . .'

Adam! Peggy glanced sharply at the woman
whose frown cleared to another smile.

'I'm sorry, that was stupid of me. Of course you
don't know us,' the woman said indulgently, not at
all put off by Peggy's coolness. 'Let me introduce
everyone.'

To Peggy's further confusion, four people in the
next row turned around to smile at her. The man
directly in front of her was stunningly handsome,
blond, blue-eyed, and with the classical features of a

Greek god. Beside him was an equally striking woman, her bright red hair organised in magnificent disarray. Next to her sat a blonde woman whose same classical beauty marked her as sister to the Greek god, and finally a dark-haired youth whose brilliant black eyes sparkled interest at Peggy.

'This is my brother-in-law, Tony Knight, his wife, Cass, his sister, Miranda, and brother, Peter. Beside me are my husband's parents, Edward and Annabel Knight . . .'

Peggy's dazed eyes acknowledged each introduction as her mind fought disbelief. 'And you must be Jenny Ross,' she said weakly.

'Well, yes, but I prefer Jenny Knight,' the woman corrected in a sweetly self-effacing manner. 'Adam asked us to look after you if you turned up.'

Miranda grinned at Peggy. 'I sure wish I'd seen that Ross Elliot Show. Jenny said you gave Adam heaps. Next time my husband gets a bit chauvinist I'm going to threaten him with that barefoot-pregnant-kitchen line. Great stuff, Peggy! But then I'm a bit of a feminist too.'

'Miranda's husband was tied up with business and couldn't get away so she flew home without him,' Jenny informed her.

'Wouldn't miss tonight for anything,' Miranda declared with relish.

'You only came to see if you could find some fault,' Tony teased his sister.

'Not true,' Miranda retorted. 'Rob wouldn't direct anything less than perfection.'

'Robert's my husband,' Jenny murmured proudly. 'He's backstage directing the traffic, and probably throwing fits. He's been impossibly tense all day.'

'If you'd seen the dress rehearsal last night, you'd be worried too,' Tony rumbled.

'Adam's a professional. He won't let us down tonight,' Cass said with confidence. 'Besides, Peggy's here.'

'What . . .' The word came out as a squeak and Peggy swallowed hard. She was absolutely floored by the distinguished company around her, and she had to fight hard not to feel intimidated. 'What has my being here got to do with anything?' she asked in a fair attempt at nonchalance.

Edward Knight leaned forward with an amused little smile. 'My dear, when a woman shows she's not impressed with a man, it's only natural for the man to want to prove her wrong. I'm sure we can look forward to an outstanding performance tonight.'

'But I didn't . . . he wouldn't even know I'm here,' Peggy pointed out, flustered by the assumptions being made.

'He'd know by now,' Jenny assured her with a smile ' which held a suggestive amount of satisfaction.

Peggy suddenly recalled the rather personal attention of the usher and wondered if he had been given instructions to relay her arrival to Adam Gale. She shrank back inside herself, embarrassed by the spotlight of Adam's interest.

'May I say that I've loved all your songs, Mrs

Knight,' she offered, somewhat self-consciously.

'Thank you.' Delight glowed from her eyes. 'But please call me Jenny. We're all making free with your name.'

Peggy saw what Adam had meant about Jenny Ross's face. It seemed to spring alive with each different expression; delight was followed by dancing amusement.

'I'm sure you'll appreciate Adam's music tonight. Mine's more for listening, his really hits you in performance. Adam has what my husband calls dramatic power. But you'll soon see that for yourself.'

Tony Knight slewed around in his seat and eyed her sternly. 'Don't let Adam blind you to everything else. I happen to be very proud of the sets I designed and I'll be seriously offended if you don't notice them.'

'And mine. I did half of them,' Cass reminded him archly.

'And hers,' he echoed mockingly. 'Though you could hardly miss hers. They jump out at you. Ow!' His face contorted in a howl of pain.

Cass turned a bland face to Peggy. 'Just ignore him. He has to be gently kicked occasionally to keep him sufferable.'

The dark-haired youth, Peter, swivelled around with a friendly grin. 'If you want to enjoy this show like any normal person, sit next to me. I won't talk music and art at you all night.'

'No, he'll just reduce the whole thing to mathematics,' Miranda shot in.

Peter was preparing to retort when the voice of

paternal authority spoke. 'That's enough, you children.'

'Children!' They both glared at their father, and turned their huffy backs to him.

Jenny's gurgle of laughter invited Peggy to share her amusement. 'Take no notice of them. They're always having a dig at each other. Miranda's an actress and Peter's a maths brain.'

'Some family!' Peggy breathed.

Jenny laughed again. 'That's what I thought when I first met them, but you're like Cass so I've no doubt that you can stand up to them.'

Like Cass! Adam had said that. Cutting people down to size. Peggy frowned, not particularly liking that image of herself. She preferred to think she gave credit where credit was due. 'Why do you say I'm like Cass?'

Jenny's eyes lit with admiration. 'All that marvellous self-confidence! I was dying for Adam to pick you on the Ross Elliot Show, and I'm so pleased you came tonight so I could meet you.'

'You meet me?' Peggy shook her head, unable to contain her incredulity. 'But I'm the one who's honoured to meet you.'

'Honoured! What nonsense! As you can see, I'm perfectly ordinary.'

Peggy had to laugh to release some of her sense of hysteria. Her much-vaunted self-confidence could not quite cope with this situation. It would be different if she and Adam were on good terms. Her pleasure at meeting all these talented people would have been immense, but as it was, she could not feel comfortable about their warm acceptance, it was as if she had entered their charmed circle under false pretences. Yet Adam had arranged it. She fingered the torn half of her ticket, trying to recall exactly what he had said when he had dropped the envelope on the bench ... something about giving her pleasure to make up for the pain.

A high-pitched drone broke her concentration.

'There's the warning-bell,' Jenny remarked, a lilt of anticipation in her voice 'not long now'.

Peggy glanced around. She had been so distracted by the Knight family that she had not noticed people filing in, but there were only a few seats left vacant in the stalls. The buzz of talk carried a charge of excitement. Peggy became more acutely aware of the magic which was special to a première. It was not only the glittering glamour of the patrons but the exhilarating sense of anticipation which attends the unveiling of a new creation. She thought of the remarkable talents which had been harnessed to make this musical a theatrical triumph and felt a tingling thrill run through her blood.

Jenny heaved a sigh. 'Oh dear! I'm getting nervous.'

Peggy flashed her a commiserating smile, although it seemed absurd that this musical genius should be nervous about her work.

The orchestra filed into the pit. There was a muted cacophony of sound as the musicians checked the tuning of their instruments. The conductor took his stand, then the lights dimmed.

'Here we go,' Jenny breathed.

Peggy saw Edward Knight reach over and give Jenny's hand a tight squeeze. A lump of emotion

rose in her own throat. This was it . . . the moment
that Adam and Jenny Ross had worked towards for
two years. And she was here, sharing it with them.
She was glad now that she had come. This was
worth any amount of heartache. Not that her heart
was aching now. It leapt with the first fanfare of
trumpets and began accelerating as drums built
momentum to a clash of cymbals. The orchestra
came surging in with theme after theme, aggression
contrasting with sweet melody, then a subtle
mingling of the two and a gradual soaring to a
triumphant climax.

Silence. Peggy could feel the audience holding its
collective breath. The drums began rolling again.
The lead-in for the 'Blind Date' song began. The
curtains opened and the stage burst into eye-
popping colour. Against a background of royal
blue, purple, navy and black, dancers whirled in
sharp, geometric patterns, their costumes a dazzling
mixture of hot pink, lime green, yellow, aqua,
violet; an ever-changing kaleidoscope, while Adam
stood above them on a glowing dais, perfectly still, a
charismatic figure in glittering white.

The music grew louder, wilder, suddenly crashing
into violent discord. The dancers froze into a
frenetic tableau as Adam broke into movement,
stalking around in obvious frustration as his voice
stabbed at the audience, explosively emotional. His
gaze swept the audience and came to a steady focus
. . . straight at Peggy.

It was just a song: a song that had been written
long before Adam had ever met her. But despite the
insistent logic in her mind, Peggy could not shake

her emotional reaction to it. Adam sang the words directly to her, loading them with such personal meaning that Peggy's heart felt squeezed.

It was not until the haunting strains of Cindy Jones' 'Dreaming' song coiled its hypnotic chords into her consciousness that Peggy even realised that the show had moved on. The stage was no longer dazzling with primary colour, but bathed in a soft light which shimmered over a set that created the perfect backdrop for a young girl's dreams ... all soft rose and gleaming silver and pale, pale blue. Because she was already emotionally disturbed, the poignant longing written into the music by Jenny Ross squeezed Peggy's heart even further.

The production never once let the audience go. The story, the music, the scenery, the singing, acting and dancing; all combined to cast a spell which held everyone in thrall with the magic on the stage. A fairy-story perhaps, but told with a mastery which gave it vibrant meaning and tugged at the heartstrings of everyone in the theatre. As the curtains closed for the interval a thunderous applause broke out, acclaiming the show a resounding success, even at its halfway point.

Peggy turned impulsively to Jenny Ross. 'It's brilliant! You really know ... understand just how to ...'

She was interrupted by Tony who turned around to Jenny with a happy grin. 'Not bad, huh?'

She laughed, a short tinkle of relief. 'Not too bad.'

'Well, not bad for something as hackneyed as Cinderella,' Peter chimed in with youthful disdain.

Miranda cuffed him.

'I loved every minute of it,' their mother declared with feeling.

'So did I,' her husband smiled, and it was perfectly obvious that the elderly couple were still very much in love with each other.

Cass rose to her feet and faced around to Peggy who was rapidly blinking to clear the tears of sentiment from her eyes. 'Looks like it got to you too,' she said with amused satisfaction.

Peggy shook her head, not in denial, but at a loss for words to describe how she felt. 'I've never seen anything so wonderfully integrated, so totally right.'

Tony eyed her sternly. 'The sets?'

'The sets captured each mood to perfection,' Peggy answered happily. 'And the music . . .' She looked at Jenny with open admiration.

'Half of it's Adam's, you know,' Jenny reminded her. 'He gave an electric performance, didn't you think?'

'Yes.' Peggy could not trust herself to say more. Her emotions were too close to the surface. Again and again Adam's gaze had sought her out and each time it had been to deliver a line which seemed to carry a pointed message

'Well, you'd better come with us and tell him so,' Tony suggested cheerfully, standing up with Cass.

Jenny also stood. 'Yes, he'd like that,' she said to Peggy.

'Now?' she choked out stupidly.

'We're going backstage,' Cass explained. 'Rob and Adam are hanging on our half-time verdicts.'

Peggy's mind executed a fast loop, rejecting the initial rush of embarrassment and clutching at the courage to test Adam's reaction to her presence. It was all very well for the Knights to make assumptions, but Peggy was not prepared to assume anything where Adam was concerned. She could not be sure that his performance on stage had been anything other than superb acting.

Nevertheless she rose to her feet, trying to quell the flutter of hope in her heart, telling herself that even if the meeting with Adam proved nothing, then at least she would meet Robert Knight whose acquaintance could be advantageous in her line of work. She was not altogether blind to Gavin's point of view.

Tony, Cass and Jenny beamed their pleasure at her, and Peggy had the distinct impression that she was the target of a carefully orchestrated manipulation. The Knight family wanted her to go to Adam, yet she could not imagine that Adam had asked them to bring her to him. No, it had to be their idea, and for some reason they felt very pleased with her company.

They sighted Robert Knight and Adam almost immediately, standing together in the wings, slightly apart from the bustle going on backstage. Peggy had no hesitation in identifying the director. The physical likeness to Peter Knight was unmistakable. She gave him no more than a cursory appraisal. Her eyes were drawn and held by the man next to him.

Adam was still dressed in the costume designed for the concert scene which had preceded the interval. Only a very masculine man could have worn it without looking effeminate, but on Adam it

looked exactly as it was supposed to . . . broodingly
romantic. From jewelled epaulettes a softly flowing
material had been dyed in a graduation of colour
from pale grey-blue to darkest midnight purple.
Billowing sleeves were gathered into jewelled cuffs
and a jewelled belt separated the blouson effect of
the top from the dark purple trousers which fitted so
revealingly they could almost have been called
ballet tights. The costume mixture of soft femininity and aggressive masculinity was tremendously
sexy and Peggy was aware of an increase in pulse-
rate even before those devastatingly blue eyes met
hers.

A flicker of triumph intensified the elation of his
success, and Peggy's instant reaction was to fall
back a step and regroup her defences. Triumph?
Did Adam regard her as someone to be conquered?
Was it merely ego which had deliberately set out to
draw this surrender from her? As if her wariness
had been telegraphed to him, Adam recomposed his
face into a polite mask. A host of inhibitions
crowded Peggy's heart as Tony, Cass and Jenny
rushed into speech, firing comments at the two
men. Robert Knight hugged Jenny to his side.
'Happy, my love?' he asked softly.

She glowed up at him. 'It's truly beautiful,
Robert. I'm so proud.'

He smiled and lifted his brilliant black eyes to
Peggy, who had been watching them in withdrawn
silence, too unsure of her position to say anything.

'Is no one going to introduce us?' he asked with
an amused lilt, his voice very like his father's.

Adam spoke. 'Peggy, this is Robert Knight.

Peggy Dean, Rob.' His tone was completely expressionless, telling her nothing.

'What did you think, Peggy? We're all too close to it to see objectively.'

'Mr Knight . . .'

'Let's make that Robert.' The black eyes crinkled in a warm offer of friendship.

Inwardly Peggy squirmed. It was impossible to respond in like manner with Adam looking on. But she had been asked for an opinion and she gave it, honestly and fairly.

'It must have been like having a dream come true to be able to work with the best anyone could offer. You had the perfect materials to create this show and I can't imagine it being presented with greater impact. You've done a brilliant job of direction. Every moment was a sensory assault on the audience. You captured them with the opening scene and you never let them go, not even for a second.'

'I?' he questioned in twinkling bemusement. 'Surely you mean Adam.'

'No, she means you,' Adam answered drily. 'Peggy's field of study is audio-visual communication. It's your work that interests her most.'

'Is that so?' Robert said with every evidence of pleasure. 'Then we must find time to talk about it, Peggy. Are you coming to the party?'

'Please excuse us for a few moments,' Adam cut in neatly, and with one hand firmly clasping her elbow, he steered Peggy away from the group. 'There's a party after the show tonight, part-publicity, part-celebration,' he muttered in her ear.

'Rob means it, Peggy. He could help you when you're ready to start looking for a job.'

She felt hopelessly confused—the kindness of the Knight family and now Adam's concern for her future career! And she was trembling inside from his physical closeness. On top of all that was the strain of not even knowing why all this was happening to her. In a burst of self-assertiveness Peggy jerked her elbow out of Adam's grasp and confronted him face to face.

'Will you please tell me what's going on?' she demanded, eyes flashing determinedly above highly flushed cheeks. 'This . . . this business with the Knight family . . . why?'

His eyes probed hers intently for several moments before he spoke. 'I wanted to please you. I thought you'd like to meet Jenny . . . if you came.'

'Yes. She's . . . she's a lovely person. Thank you. But they're all . . .' She looked at him uncertainly. 'They're all being so nice to me, and they seem to think . . . well, that you . . . and I . . .'

He sighed and his mouth took on an ironic twist. 'I'm sorry if you feel embarrassed by their interest. I made these arrangements before I saw you last night. I would have told you about them but I got the impression you wouldn't come anyway.'

The tension of their last meeting was curling around them, threatening the tenuous line of communication.

'I'm glad you did come,' Adam said softly.

Peggy took a deep breath to steady her galloping pulse. 'So am I. It was very kind of you to bring me the ticket. And sitting me with the Knights.'

Adam hesitated a moment, his eyes sharply appraising. 'Would you like to come to the party, Peggy?'

'I think . . .' She swallowed hard to moisten a very dry throat. 'I think I'd feel out of place by myself.'

There was an excruciating silence before Adam spoke again, and the eyes that challenged hers held a steely glint of pride. 'Would you come with me?'

Her heart turned over. It was true, he did want another chance. His performance on stage had been a pointed plea to her. And her own desire dictated her answer. 'Yes.'

The polite mask was broken by a smile and the reserve in his eyes melted into a warmth which tingled into Peggy's soul. 'Jenny will bring you around to my dressing-room after the show,' he said eagerly.

'I'd like that,' she agreed, not even stopping to think what she was agreeing to, knowing only that she wanted another chance too.

'Adam! Time you were changing,' Robert Knight called out with firm authority.

'I'm on my way.' He took Peggy's hand in his and squeezed it gently. 'Thank you for coming tonight. It meant a lot to me, knowing you were here. I hope you enjoy the rest of the show as much as you did the first half.'

She could not let his generosity go unmatched. 'Adam . . .' She forced the truth through a wave of self-consciousness, hoping he would accept it at its face-value and not think she was flattering him. 'You really are a great performer.'

A wide grin lit his face with happiness. 'It was for you.'

She mulled over those words as he led her back to the others. Was her approval important to Adam? He had claimed that her presence meant a lot to him, but how much? That was the really prickly question because Peggy knew that in accepting his invitation to the party, she was playing with fire as far as her own emotions were concerned.

'Jenny, will you lead Peggy to me after the show?'

'Delighted to,' Jenny smiled, linking her arm with Peggy's as Adam waved a cheery salute and moved off.

Peggy wished there had been more time to talk to him. So little had been said, and a great deal had been left unsaid. But perhaps it was better this way. A truce had been negotiated by actions rather than words, and Peggy had to concede that the actions had been very generous. Where Adam intended them to lead was an unanswerable question as yet, but she wanted to find out. And tonight would be a start. Maybe a new start, she hoped.

CHAPTER EIGHT

ADAM handed her into the back seat of the limousine and climbed in after her. The door was shut and the uniformed chauffeur paced his dignified way to the driver's side and took his place behind the wheel. The car slid into motion with a barely perceptible purr. A glass partition separated driver from passengers and for the first time since the show had ended, Peggy was effectively alone with Adam.

His dressing-room had been the centre of hectic coming and going, a seemingly endless stream of people showering Adam with compliments and generally expressing their jubilation at the success of the musical. The audience had applauded through seven curtain-calls, ample proof that they had been royally entertained and the king of pop was undoubtedly a megastar tonight. No Range Rover or tracksuit or Harry's Place for this Adam Gale . . . a limousine, the formal tailoring of an elegant dinner-suit, and a party at the city Hilton Hotel.

Peggy sat beside him in her three-year-old houndstooth coat and wondered what she had let herself in for. Up until tonight she had completely disregarded Adam's stardom, but there was no disregarding it now. He was not just any ordinary person. He was brilliantly talented; he belonged to

the world and the world acclaimed him, as well it
should. But somehow the acclaim seemed to have
dwarfed any significance she could have in his life.
She glanced at him questioningly, wanting to break
the silence between them but wishing he would
speak first.

The blue eyes held sympathy. 'Are you finding all
this a bit daunting?'

'Not daunting so much as ... well, I guess it's
seeing you from a different point of view. Now I
know why you have fans swooning over you. You
really were marvellous, Adam. Compelling. Dyna-
mic. All the words that everyone has used.' Her
smile held a touch of irony. 'I can see it would be a
crime to keep you barefoot, pregnant and chained
to the kitchen.'

He laughed, his eyes dancing over her with
pleasure.

'You must feel tremendously elated at how well it
all went,' Peggy added.

His grin slowly died into a sigh. 'Yes, it's great!'
He took her hand in his and fondled it while he
spoke on, a gentle self-mockery creeping into his
voice. 'It's great while you're doing it and great for a
little while afterwards, and then it's nothing.
Because it's not real, Peggy. It doesn't last. When
the show is over and the people have gone home,
you're left with yourself, and you're not a star any
more. You're just a person, alone, in a hotel room.
And however sumptuous the furnishings, the room
is hauntingly empty.'

His gaze dropped to their hands. He threaded his
fingers through hers and gripped tightly. 'The

temptation is to keep the high going as long as you can because you don't want to face that loneliness. So you take a girl who wants you to fulfil her fantasy and you're a star for a little while longer. But all you've done is given another performance and the loneliness afterwards is even worse.'

He lifted his gaze to hers, revealing a vulnerability which softened the harsh edges of the picture he had drawn. 'You said you acknowledged the fact that no one is perfect. I know I'm far from perfect and I've done a hell of a lot of regrettable things in my life, but none more regrettable than walking out on you. I felt that what we had going between us that afternoon was real, more real than anything I've had with any other woman.'

His mouth twisted into a rueful grimace. 'Which is why I reacted so savagely when . . .' He shook his head as if wanting to erase the memory, then shot her an intense look of appeal. 'It was a hell of a thing to do. Can you forgive me the greatest idiocy of my life?'

Her smile reassured him. 'I guess I wouldn't be here if I hadn't forgiven you, Adam.'

He lifted her hand and his mouth grazed across her knuckles. The blue eyes were almost hypnotic in their compelling desire. 'Stay with me tonight and I swear I'll make it up to you, Peggy.'

The invitation . . . command . . . brought a twanging tension to every nerve in her body. Her mind winced away from the starkness of those words and yet . . . wasn't that why she was here? Logic forced her to face up to the undeniable fact that she did want Adam Gale but a whole tumult of emotions warred against logic. Not like this . . . not like this, they cried. Being with him . . . yes . . . but not just for a satisfying sexual experience. She wanted . . .

Adam moved. His hand curved around her burning cheek and turned her face up to his. He was so close, only inches away. And he spoke softly, seductively, and his eyes bored into hers, willing away the turmoil in her heart.

'It won't be like the last time, Peggy, I promise you. I'll make it as beautiful as it should be. I want to give you everything you ever dreamed of.'

And he kissed her with such tenderness that her turmoil melted into an overwhelming desire to meet his need. Her lips pressed an instinctive invitation and, encouraged by her response, Adam deepened the kiss to one of sensual persuasion. Peggy was powerless to resist any overture he might have made, and if circumstances had not intervened, she would have given him everything he wanted of her.

The car bumped a little and tilted upwards. Adam abruptly pulled away. He threw a sharp glance out the window, snatched the handkerchief from his top pocket and began rubbing his mouth with it, removing all trace of her lipstick. The action seemed such an insulting rejection of her that Peggy shrank away from him, hurt and shocked by the sheer cold-bloodedness of his withdrawal. It was a chilling repetition of what he had done to her before . . . promising her love then casting her aside. Her shiver of revulsion snapped Adam's attention back to her.

'No!' He caught her hands in urgent re-posses-
sion. 'Don't look like that! We're on the ramp
leading up to the main foyer of the hotel. The press
will be waiting to pounce on us.'

'Would it be so terrible if they knew you had
kissed me, Adam?' she asked stonily.

He frowned and gave a sharp, negative shake of
the head. 'You don't understand. They're like
piranhas. Give them a crumb and they'll make a
meal of you.' He pressed her hands tightly. His eyes
pleaded against the reserve in hers. 'Our private
lives are our own, Peggy. I don't want to share what
we have with the press.'

'Then what am I supposed to be to you? In the
public eye,' she added pointedly.

'If we don't tell them, they won't know. The only
way to keep them at bay is to give nothing away.
Please trust me, Peggy. I've had years of this and I
know how best to handle them.'

The hurt was not completely assuaged but there
was no time left to pursue the matter. The limousine
had pulled up at the entrance doors and already a
group of men were rushing forward, some lifting
cameras in readiness.

Adam squeezed her hands again. 'Trust me,' he
begged, the blue eyes intent on reaching into her
heart once more.

She nodded, but her heart was still pumping an
instinctive protest. The feeling of being publicly
disowned by him persisted, despite Adam's explanation. However, she felt a little better when Adam
draped a protective arm around her shoulders as she
stepped out of the car. Flashlights popped. Adam

swept her into the foyer at a fast pace, heading straight for the bank of elevators. Their progress was impeded as reporters dodged around in front of them, flinging out a barrage of questions.

'A formal interview will be given upstairs, gentlemen,' Adam stated politely. 'Please move aside.'

'The girl with you . . . isn't she the one you picked on the Ross Elliot Show?'

'What's your relationship?'

'No comment,' Adam said tersely.

'Miss Dean, what did you think of Adam's performance?'

'Miss Dean, is Adam Gale better than a stereo-set?'

Peggy blushed to the roots of her hair. It was awful that her own words could be given such a suggestive twist. Even when they reached an open elevator they were given no respite. Some members of the press pursued them into it and persisted with questions.

'You are straining my good humour, gentlemen,' Adam remarked quietly. 'You were informed of the arrangements.'

'Oh, come on, Adam. It's not often we catch you with a girl in tow,' one complained.

'*Lady*. Miss Dean is a lady,' Adam corrected pointedly. 'And I'd be obliged if you'd respect her as such.'

Pens scribbled. They had been given a quote and when the elevator-doors opened, Adam and Peggy were allowed to step out and proceed unhindered. Adam smiled down at her with a hint of smugness which suggested he had proved his point but Peggy was not so sure. She agreed that their relationship was no one's business but their own. Indeed, she herself had blocked Gavin's speculation at every turn, but the press was not going to be blocked. For the lack of anything definitive, speculation and innuendo would be printed, and Peggy found that idea more distasteful than an honest declaration of interest from Adam ... if he was honestly interested.

But there was no time to question the confusion in her heart. Adam led her into a large room full of people, and his appearance was greeted by a spontaneous burst of applause. He responded with a graceful wave of acknowledgement and steered Peggy towards the Knight family which formed the nucleus of a milling crowd. Adam was immediately enveloped in the euphoria of success, welcomed, fêted, toasted with gallons of champagne. Peggy stood beside him and smiled until her face ached.

She lost count of the number of women who threw their arms around Adam and planted congratulatory kisses all over his beaming face. He certainly did not mind the press witnessing those kisses, she thought caustically, then chided herself for being unreasonable. It wasn't only Adam being kissed. Karen Ester, the girl who had played Cindy Jones, and Jenny Ross were both receiving the same exuberant benedictions, and they too, indeed everyone around them were bubbling over with excitement. Tony Knight was tossing off an endless stream of wisecracks which Cass developed with ever-increasing hilarity. Miranda and Peter were stirring them on. Everywhere Peggy looked, everyone seemed to be in scintillating spirits.

Particularly Gavin. He had wasted no time in getting himself introduced around. To Peggy's private surprise he had made no comment at all on her presence, not even an uplifted eyebrow. He was all too delighted at having gained acceptance into the company of so many celebrities.

She watched him circulating purposefully, making the most of his opportunities. There were many people who could wield influence in this room and Peggy wondered if it was stupid of her not to curry favour with them while she had the chance. Adam certainly did not need her at his side. She doubted if he would even miss her. But such a move went against the grain of her character.

'So the stars were right after all.'

The drawled insinuation close to Peggy's ear startled her even more than the arm sliding around her shoulders. She turned her head sharply and almost caught Ross Elliot's chin. He chuckled at her surprise, and seemed vastly amused to see her in Adam's company.

'I think you owe me another show, Peggy Dean. You've obviously got more from the last one than was your due.' His eyes crinkled up at Adam. 'How about it? A return performance, so to speak. You got good footage out of the competition.'

Adam laughed. 'I'm not sure Peggy would appreciate that point, Ross. Let it ride.'

'Great show, Adam. If you want to give the bookings a boost, you're welcome on my programme any time. You too, Peggy.' He gave her a teasing grin. 'You and Adam are as good a vaudeville act as one can find these days.'

Adam's attention was claimed once again by more well-wishers. Peggy only just managed to smother an exasperated grimace but the tightening of her face had been noticed by Ross Elliot as he withdrew his arm. He wagged a teasing finger at her.

'Love, not war,' he murmured provocatively before drifting off.

Love! Was this mad physical desire that Adam awakened in her . . . love? Was what he felt for her even remotely connected to love? He wanted her in his bed tonight to take away the loneliness when the party was over. For all the attention he was paying to her now, he might as well have asked her to go straight to his bedroom and wait.

Here the court was playing homage to its king. She stood beside him but she was not a recognised or acknowledged consort. She was merely the girl at Adam's side on this particular night, a position that many a girl had held before her. Lip-service courtesy had been extended to her but she had no real identity here, not in her own right, nor given to her by Adam. He had withheld that right on the dubious grounds of privacy.

She smothered a sigh as the bleak thought came to her that she was a fool to be here at all. One afternoon . . . that was all she had spent with him, and more likely than not, she was a novelty to him, a challenge, a conquest that had not been completed to his satisfaction. Her heart twisted with self-torment. Should she go . . . put this infatuation

behind her and forget it? Surely that was all it was
... infatuation?

'I think Robert's about to set up the press
interview, Adam.' It was Edward Knight and he
turned his attention to Peggy, his smile telling her
that she was not a mere consort to him. 'Peggy,
would you be so kind as to join me at the buffet? I'm
sure Adam's been too occupied to look after you
properly. We can pick over the food and find a table
where we can rest our feet for a while.'

'Thank you, Mr Knight. I'd like that very much,'
Peggy replied warmly, touched by his
thoughtfulness.

'I'm sorry, Peggy,' Adam said with a quick
frown. 'I didn't think of food.'

'It doesn't matter. You've had no time.' No time
for me either, she added silently. The frown
deepened and she flashed him a brittle smile.
Perhaps this was the opportunity she should take to
slip away. She wondered if Adam would even notice
her departure—not until he wanted to leave, she
decided cynically. 'Go and do your interview and
don't worry about me.'

'Why should he worry?' Edward Knight demanded lightly. 'I'm no competition.'

Adam's face cleared to a grin. 'I wouldn't say
that, Edward. It's only because you're married to
Annabel that I'd let Peggy go with you.'

'You young men still have a lot to learn,' was the
wise retort as he patted Adam on the shoulder and
turned to steer Peggy away.

The room was luxuriously fitted out in a cabaret
style. The band playing from a small stage had

apparently been instructed to keep the music to background level. No one had made use of the dance-floor, and despite the number of tables and chairs, few people had remained seated for long.

An elaborate *smörgasbord* had been set out on one long table and it had been picked over by guests at their leisure. Drink waiters had been continually circulating, quick to serve everyone's needs. Peggy had downed a dizzying amount of champagne and common sense advised a solid meal to dilute some of its effect. Edward Knight handed her a large plate and took the same size for himself.

'Nothing like a good lining on the stomach to get you through an evening like this,' he remarked drily.

Peggy smiled at him. 'Don't tell me you're not enjoying yourself.'

'Too well, my dear. I shall soon be making a fool of myself if I'm not careful.' She threw him a sceptical look as she helped herself to some ham and chicken. 'Somehow I can't imagine that.'

His eyes twinkled. 'I feel myself teetering on the brink, and I'm counting on you to sober me up. You have a very sharp mind.'

'What makes you think so?' Peggy asked, amused by his gallant manner.

'I watched the Ross Elliot Show with Jenny.'

Peggy rolled her eyes. She wished she had never gone on the damned show. 'I wasn't too sharp that day, Mr Knight. I got all my calculations wrong.'

He chuckled and pointed to an empty table. Their plates were now laden with appetising food and they sat themselves down to enjoy their meal.

Peggy's stomach felt quite hollow and despite her inner depression, she found a hearty appetite.

'I would like to take issue with one of your replies to Adam's questions,' Edward Knight remarked casually.

She darted him a wry look. 'I've already recanted the barefoot-pregnant-kitchen one. Adam undoubtedly belongs on a stage.'

He smiled and shook his head. 'You declared you wouldn't do anything to make the man in your life feel special. But you see, Peggy, everyone wants to feel special, particularly the ones we love. That's what makes love stick. If you're not prepared to give that feeling to anyone, then you'll never achieve a lasting relationship.'

He paused then softly added, 'It's not propping up an ego, my dear, it's giving emotional security. And I'm sorry to see that Adam has failed to give it to you at this party tonight.'

She looked into the perceptive dark eyes and knew that he knew. 'Yes,' she admitted frankly. It was something of a relief to speak to someone who understood her emotional dilemma. 'He doesn't need me here.'

A dry little smile mocked her assertion. 'If he doesn't need you, why did he ask you?'

Peggy frowned, mulling over Edward Knight's logic, but finally dismissing it as she recalled Adam's revelations in the car. 'It's more complex than that. Something he has to prove maybe . . . I'm not sure. I wish I was.'

The old man nodded. 'You're strongly attracted to him.'

She shrugged. 'What woman wouldn't be?'

'No, I don't mean that. You would have been trying to win the date with him if Adam's obvious attributes had meant anything to you.'

'I think you know too much, Mr Knight,' Peggy commented ruefully.

'Age and experience, my dear, and both of them tell me that it would take a woman of very strong character to forge a successful relationship with Adam Gale. He's a man who's stood alone for a long time. He needs to be taught what is required from him.'

She watched him consume the last morsel from his plate and neatly set down his knife and fork. The dark gaze lifted to hers, measuring her reaction to his words.

'What would you advise me to do?' Peggy asked bluntly.

His eyes softened to a warm approval. 'I wouldn't presume to advise you, Peggy. I have merely been speaking of things I know to be true. Sometimes a little talking helps to clear the mind so it can choose a direction.' He paused, then spoke with more emphasis. 'I think anything worth having is worth fighting for. It's up to you to decide what you want, my dear.'

Peggy finished her own meal, chewing over those last words in her mind. Before Edward Knight had intervened she had almost decided that it would be foolish to pursue a relationship with Adam. She was not prepared to fill the role of background girl. Pride had insisted that it would never satisfy her. But the truth which had brought her to the theatre tonight was still pulsing in her heart. No other man had evoked desire in her nor churned her emotions into such a state of confusion.

'Have you always got what you fought for, Mr Knight?' she asked curiously.

He smiled acknowledgement of her point. 'No, but I've always had the satisfaction of knowing I tried every avenue possible. And I did get what I wanted most.' His gaze turned to where his wife was chatting with Cass's mother, and his face settled into lines of contentment.

Peggy's gaze travelled further, to the end of the room where the stage had been vacated by the band and chairs had been set out for the formal press interview. Adam was leading Karen Ester to the central pair of chairs. He was smiling at his beautiful co-star and Peggy felt a swift stab of jealousy. But Adam had not asked Karen Ester or any other woman to ride to this party with him. He had asked Peggy. That meant something, didn't it? He wanted her ... Peggy Dean. And yes, she wanted him. She was not going to walk away.

'I see that they're about to begin the interviews,' Edward Knight remarked, turning back to Peggy. 'Shall we join the audience?'

Everyone was moving forward to listen to the question/answer session. Peggy's shaky confidence received a boost when Adam looked down the room, directly at her, seeming to ask for her interest. She flashed him a brilliant smile and stood up. 'Yes, let's hear what they have to say,' she said brightly to Edward Knight.

The old man rose to his feet and offered his arm.

Peggy took it and gave it an impulsive hug. 'Thank you for talking to me.'

A gleam of satisfaction shone out of the all-too-knowledgeable eyes. 'It's always a pleasure to talk with a woman of character,' was the warm reply. 'I hope we'll meet again.' Peggy hoped so too. She hoped to share in every facet of Adam's life, including his friendship with the remarkable Knight family, but right now her first priority was to stamp her own presence on Adam's consciousness. Indelibly. If she had to fight, then fight she would. Through every possible avenue. And suddenly her heart was pumping very strongly indeed.

CHAPTER NINE

ADAM fielded the questions aimed at him with the same smooth professionalism he had exhibited on the Ross Elliot Show. He was charming, generous in his praise of others, drily humorous . . . handling the pressure of the spotlight with the ease of long experience. Only at the end did his performance falter.

One reporter had the temerity to bring up Peggy's name again. Adam's face tightened. He lifted a disdainful eyebrow at the offender and his smile was very, very cool. 'Since you have no more questions about the show, let's call it a night, gentlemen. Thank you for coming.'

He stood on the last word and helped Karen to her feet. Taking their cue with barely a pause, Robert and Tony followed suit, supporting Jenny and Cass as they all took a bow to appreciative applause. Their solidarity allowed no demur from the press, who had been given ample material for any number of stories.

Once off the stage, Adam separated from the group and headed straight for Peggy. 'That bloody scandal-monger will be barred from any press conference I hold in the future,' he muttered fiercely, then softened his voice to apology. 'I'm sorry about that. There's always some ferret who can't play fair, but I promise you I'll protect you all I can, Peggy.' The blue eyes searched hers anxiously. 'All right?'

She would have preferred him to have answered the reporter's question openly and honestly, but she realised that Adam had divided his life into compartments, and right now she did not have the power to knock the walls down. She smiled reassurance. 'I guess it's the price one pays for being with you. I hope it's worth it,' she added on a note of challenge.

A gleam of arrogance dispelled the anxiety. 'Have you had enough of this party?'

'More to the point, have you?' she retorted drily. 'It's your affair.'

A quick frown indicated a jarring of confidence. 'Didn't you enjoy it, Peggy? I thought most girls liked this sort of thing.'

'I'm not most girls, remember?' she flashed back at him, pride sharpening her tongue before her earlier resolution could overtake the response.

Pride stiffened his voice. 'I'm sorry it was such a trial to you.'

She breathed a sigh of exasperation at her lack of control. Was she always going to react emotionally to Adam? It was his big night, and deservedly so. Did she have to go and spoil it for him? With renewed purpose she softened her voice. 'Maybe it was a trial of what I can expect with you in public, but I'm still here, Adam.'

Again the quick frown. 'I thought you'd be glad of the opportunity to meet some of the big names in television.'

Her eyes gently mocked his assumption. 'Don't

confuse me with Gavin. There's only one important person in this room as far as I'm concerned, and it might be selfish of me, but I'm rather tired of sharing him with everyone else.'

The smile Adam gave her was the best reward Peggy had ever received for effort of any kind. She had made him feel uniquely special and pure, undiluted pleasure beamed down at her, wrapping her in a warm glow. The desire which slowly kindled in the brilliant blue gaze found a ready echo in her own galloping pulse.

'Let's get out of here,' he breathed and his grasp on her waist was decidedly possessive as he swept her along with him, only pausing to collect her coat and handbag.

Had Adam felt as uncertain with her as she had with him? Peggy wondered, then realised that her fierce rejection to his apologetic overture on the previous night could hardly have generated confidence.

As if responding to Adam's will a set of elevator doors opened on the press of the first button and he whirled her inside, stabbing at more buttons on the way. The doors closed and Peggy barely had a moment to register their movement upwards. She was in Adam's arms, pressed to the whole urgent length of him.

'You don't know how good it feels to have you with me, Peggy. I've been worrying myself sick about you these last two weeks.'

The genuine feeling which roughened his voice convinced Peggy that he was speaking the truth. She had been as much on his mind as he had been

on hers. She wound her arms around his neck in a
pliant surrender to her own need. 'You haven't been
out of my thoughts either.'

'Bad thoughts?'

'Some. But mostly wishing it had been different.'

'It will be.' His eyes darkened with some
indefinable but intense emotion. 'It will be with
you.'

Her heart gave a joyful little leap. Surely he was
telling her that she was special to him too?

The elevator slid to a halt and opened on to a
wide, lushly carpeted corridor. Adam hurried Peggy
out and along to an impressive set of oak doors. He
quickly unlocked one and ushered her inside.
Peggy's high-heels clacked loudly on the marble
floor of a small foyer. Adam took her elbow and
steered her into what could only be called a luxury
apartment.

The pale peach décor was the last word in
elegance and Peggy's gaze swivelled slowly around,
taking in all the evidence of no-expense-spared
living quarters. Sofa and armchairs set around a
brass-topped coffee-table, television, video and
stereo-sets, an antique writing desk, large dining
table and accompanying chairs, a fully equipped
bar, beautiful lamps, resplendent plants and ferns
in gleaming pots, a spiral staircase leading to an
upper floor ... Peggy had only ever seen such
settings in movies and magazines.

'Do you live here?' she choked out, a little
overwhelmed by her surroundings.

'God, no!' Adam laughed. 'I just took it for the
night.'

She turned on him in amazement, her frugal
mind staggered by such extravagance. 'All this just
for one night?'

Adam was discarding his dinner-jacket. He
tossed it over the nearest chair and grinned at her as
he began undoing his bow-tie. 'I can afford it,
Peggy.'

'But why stay here when you can easily go home?'
she asked in puzzlement.

'For convenience's sake.' His grin turned a little
crooked. 'If you hadn't come tonight I would've had
the party continue up here and probably drunk
myself blind in the process.'

Peggy's heart leapt again at what seemed a
further proof of emotional involvement with her.
'Gavin said you did that last night,' she remarked
questioningly.

Adam's eyebrows rose, then formed an irritated
V. 'I didn't expect him to tell you about that.'

'Why did you go with him?' Peggy asked, not
quite prepared to accept Gavin's interpretation of
the facts without Adam's confirmation.

The bow-tie landed on the coat and Peggy's gaze
was drawn to the slow baring of flesh as Adam
unbuttoned his shirt. A little frisson of fear ran
through her veins. Did Adam mean to get fully
undressed while she stood there watching? The
fingers stopped unbuttoning halfway down his
chest and switched to removing his cuff-links and
rolling up his sleeves.

Peggy breathed a sigh of relief. She had never
been faced with the practicalities of conducting a
love affair; it was one thing to be carried away on a

wave of passion, quite another to enter into it cold-bloodedly. Adam's calm voice snapped her out of the momentary self-doubt.

'Initially I went with him because he asked me for a lift and it was something to do. Then he started talking about you and I was interested in hearing what he could tell me.' He shot her a brooding look. 'I couldn't let it rest, Peggy. I didn't come to you last night just to make myself feel better. I was concerned about what effect my actions might have had on you and . . .' he heaved a sigh and closed the distance between them, taking her gently in his arms, 'and I kept remembering what it had been like between us before I killed it.'

'You didn't kill it. The body still has life,' she said wryly, made all too aware of her physical reaction to his closeness. Even her breathing felt tight as her pulse jumped to a new tempo.

One of Adam's hands lifted, lightly cupping her cheek, and his eyes held a tender reassurance as he spoke. 'Please don't be afraid of me, Peggy.'

'I'm not afraid,' she denied quickly.

'I saw you tense a moment ago. Because I was undressing?'

Her lashes swept down, veiling the confusion aroused by his frankness. 'It's just . . . I'm not used to these situations,' she confessed weakly.

'Peggy . . .' His voice was very soft . . . sympathetic. 'I want to make love to you. I can't deny that. But I'm not totally insensitive to how you might be feeling about it. After last time. If you'd rather just talk, that's fine by me. Okay?'

He cared about her! He really did care about her.

But she did not want him viewing her as a psychiatric case of sexual repression. She wanted to meet him on equal ground and know that his caring went way beyond any guilt he was feeling. She raised her lashes and showed him the depth of that yearning. 'I want to make love with you,' she whispered huskily.

Make love . . . love . . . love . . . her heart thumped insistently as Adam's mouth closed over hers. For a moment he had hesitated, seeming to doubt that she was genuinely willing, but whatever question had crossed his mind was swiftly erased by the passion which answered him. It was not surrender she gave but a wholehearted response to every initiative he took.

Urgent, possessive hands arched her body to fit his, imprinting the provocative intimacy of his arousal on her softly pliant flesh. The warm flood of sensation which swept through her intensified the whirling excitement of his kiss, and her gasp was almost a moan of need when Adam abruptly ended it. A hand thrust into the thick curls at the back of her neck and pressed her head on to his shoulder. His chest heaved against hers as he sucked in a deep breath and she felt it whisper past her ear.

'What is it with you, Peggy?' he rasped shakily. 'You drive me to the peak of desire so fast, I can barely grasp control. And I can't take you this fast. It's got to be right for you.'

'It's right,' she murmured, pressing encouraging lips to the taut cord of muscle in his throat.

He groaned and swept his mouth over her hair again and again in an agony of longing. 'I haven't even asked if it's safe for you. I didn't ask last time. I could've got you pregrant, Peggy, did you think of that?'

'No. Not then,' she admitted, wishing he would stop talking. She didn't want to talk, she didn't want to think about what she was doing now. She just wanted him to love her.

'What about tonight?' He gentled his embrace, lessening the urgency which had been rampant need barely a few moments ago. 'I don't want you to be hurt in any way. Is it safe or should I . . .'

'No!' The word burst from her, an instinctive protest at such cool premeditation. She swallowed back more telling words, knowing she should be grateful for Adam's considerate forethought, but unable to shake the thought that Adam was making sure there could be no unwelcome comeback from this night. 'Thank you. But it's quite safe,' she said stiffly.

He sighed and his mouth curved into a smile of self-mockery. 'You make me want to protect you. I guess it kind of gets to me that you've never been with anyone. I want to give you a good memory, Peggy. No worries.'

A good memory. Was that all it was going to be? For a moment Peggy panicked, then her confidence reasserted itself. She was special to him. Different to the other women he had had. He cared about her. He was looking after her. 'I'm not worried about anything,' she declared firmly.

A soft fire glowed in his eyes, melting the last niggling doubt. 'You're beautiful, truly beautiful, Peggy Dean, and I want to savour every moment with you. No wild rush. I want it to be . . . like creating music.'

She knew how much that meant to him and a song of elation pulsed through her veins.

Adam suddenly grinned at her, his face surprisingly boyish and free of all cynicism. 'I'll get a bottle of champagne and we'll take it upstairs with us. Ever had a spa bath, Peggy?'

'No.'

'Nothing like it for getting rid of tension. And it's the best way to ease the muscles after a hard session of dancing.' He had left her to go to the bar where he was fixing an ice bucket for the champagne. He flashed her a twinkling glance as he collected two elegant flute glasses. 'You'll enjoy it.'

Peggy gulped. 'Are you telling me there's a spa bath upstairs?'

'Uh-huh. And a sauna, but I think we'll give that a miss.' With his hands occupied Adam nodded towards the spiral staircase in one corner. 'Let's go.'

The staircase led to a bedroom which more than matched the splendour of the décor downstairs. Peggy's breathing developed a decided roughness.

'Will you open the door for me, please?'

She dragged her gaze from the king-size bed and moved to the door where Adam was standing. It opened into a huge bathroom which seemed even more dazzling than the rest of the apartment. Adam set down the champagne and glasses on the tiles edging the spa bath and turned on the taps. Peggy was relieved to see that the bath was more than spacious enough to hold two people comfortably.

'I'll leave you with it while I telephone a few

instructions to Reception,' he said casually. 'Be right back.'

Peggy stared after him, too stunned to move. Did he expect her to undress? By herself? Be all naked ... ready for him when he returned? Her whole being recoiled at such a clinical start to the union of bodies and hearts she had envisaged. It cut right across any sense of togetherness.

She turned and stared at the bath. It had been a long night for Adam. A spa bath was not unreasonable before they made love; if she got in the water maybe she wouldn't feel quite so self-conscious. Obviously Adam was used to girls who thought nothing of stripping off. It was possible that he was merely being tactful, leaving her alone in case she wanted to use the other bathroom facilities. Peggy took a deep breath and undressed as fast as she could.

She lowered her trembling body into the bath and was actually beginning to enjoy the shooting streams of bubbles on her skin when Adam returned, stark naked. Her gaze skittered over his very masculine physique as he stepped in at the other end of the bath. He settled himself, grinned at her, then proceeded to pop the cork of the champagne bottle and fill the glasses. He leaned over and handed her one as naturally as if they were sitting across a table in a restaurant.

'What did Edward have to say for himself?'

Peggy struggled for a moment to focus her mind on Adam's question. The sight of him so fully revealed, had blanked out all thought while a thousand little electric charges had exploded under her skin. She recollected her faculties with some difficulty and found a relief in the fact that Adam had not referred to any features of her nudity.

'Oh, just what a grand night it had been.' she replied with a fair attempt at nonchalance. His toes had found her feet and were stroking the sensitive soles. It was all she could do not to wriggle.

'Yes, a grand night!' His smile was one of quiet triumph. 'It really captured the audience, didn't it?'

'They loved it,' Peggy affirmed. 'I think you've got a long-running show on your hands.'

'Let's drink to that,' he grinned. And they did. Adam's smile slowly faded and his eyes lost their sparkle. 'I envy Robert and Tony ... having Edward as their father. I respect him more than any man I've ever met.'

The touch of loneliness in his voice prompted Peggy to rush into speech, instinctively wanting to fill any void he might feel. 'He's a very kind man. And very astute, I think. You must enjoy your friendship with the Knight family very much, Adam.'

'Mmm ... I do. Yet they make me a little too aware of what I don't have. They're complete people ... every one of the Knights. Do you know what I mean?'

'That they've found what they want from life?'

He sipped his drink, eyeing her consideringly over the rim. 'Yes, I guess that's it.'

Peggy was conscious of a flush creeping up her neck as the speculative gleam in Adam's eyes took on a hungry edge. She sipped her own champagne, feeling the bubbles tingle over her tongue. Bubbles inside and outside, she thought whimsically, her skin tingling from the gentle bombardment of the spa. It was an extraordinarily sensual feeling. Adam's toes moved to a slow caress of her ankles, sending a crazy spasm of excitement up her legs.

'Come here,' he commanded softly.

No. Not in a bath. No. The rejection in Peggy's mind was instant and instinctive, overriding everything else. All her doubts came searing back, burning away the hope that a night spent with Adam would lead to more than a mere physical connection. This was one step too far. She had accepted the talk of contraception, and the clinical undressing, but she couldn't accept this. It reduced what they would have together to a bit of erotic sex . . . the kind Adam had undoubtedly shared before with any number of willing partners.

She surged out of the bath, whipped a towel off the nearby railing and wrapped it around her dripping body. 'Forget it, Adam!' she flung at him before swooping to pick up her clothes. 'Forget the whole damned thing!'

'What in hell!'

Peggy marched out of the bathroom, ignoring the huge splash of water behind her. She had been fooling herself, constructing a dream that could never be. Adam Gale could keep his pop-star world, she wanted no part of it.

Hands gripped her shoulders hard and spun her round: Adam's face was contorted in anger. 'Now wait a damned minute!'

'I'm not waiting for anything,' she bit out with equal anger, sparks of resentment flying from her eyes. 'I don't need your sexual expertise to make me feel better. You can take it and . . . and give it to some other girl who'll be tickled pink at making it with the great Adam Gale in a spa bath.'

'I don't want some other girl,' he grated. 'What is this? A pay-back for what I did to you? Is that it, Peggy?'

He shook her and the towel around her body came loose. Peggy tried to clutch it as it fell and half the clothes in her arms spilled to the floor as well as the towel. Horribly conscious of her nakedness Peggy lifted her chin with defiant pride and spoke with barely controlled ferocity. 'I don't care about that other time. I don't need a good memory from you to take its place. I hereby release you of any guilt you've felt over it—I don't want your guilt or anything else. Is that clear?'

She had gone too far. A wave of despairing emotion choked her and to her utter mortification, tears rushed into her eyes. She tried to jerk out of Adam's hold but he suddenly stepped forward, pulling her against him, and the slap of his naked body against hers plunged her nerves into quivering chaos.

'What about this?' Adam rasped in her ear. 'Is this nothing to you?'

His mouth burned a trail down her throat and across her shoulder and the flesh beneath its sensual pressure leapt with feverish excitement. The last of her clothes slid out of her hold, dropped as her unconscious hands lifted to curl around Adam's neck. Instantly Adam's embrace tightened, hands running down the curve of her spine, pressing her into him as if he could not bear the tiniest separation. His lips swept across her hair, his breath warm on her temples as he spoke, urgently and vehemently.

'I've never wanted any woman so much. The bath was only a prelude, Peggy. I was trying to hold off ... give you time to relax and be comfortable with me.' His fingers thrust into her curls and dragged her head back. Adam's eyes burnt into hers, commanding her surrender. 'You think this is guilt? I'm barely hanging on to control. Do you understand?'

She was trembling under the force of his desire. A melting weakness had invaded her body and she couldn't even find the strength to speak, to answer him.

'Say you want me, Peggy. Say it!'

'Yes.'

The word was only a hiss of breath but it was enough. Mouth met mouth in hungry need and fed their desire for each other with a greed which knew no bounds. Their bodies strained closer, soft flesh yielding to hard muscle, revelling in the intimacy of every physical imprint which their hands engineered, fiercely possesive.

Adam half-carried her to the bed and they fell on it together. Only then did he lift his mouth from hers, allowing them both a breathing space. Their eyes met and clung, wild, glazed eyes, mirrors of their abandonment to the desire which seethed between them, compelling a resolution. Neither spoke a word. They were beyond words.

Adam's hands grasped her breasts, pushing up

the swell of soft flesh, rolling his thumbs over the taut nipples again and again. Peggy's breath came in quick, excited gasps which degenerated into a long moan of pleasure as he bent his head and took each tingling peak in his mouth, kissing one, then the other, teasing with his tongue, driving her crazy with an erotic suction which sent wave after wave of aching sweetness through her veins.

She reached for him, hands raking his hair and shoulders; pleading, urging, frantic hands. But he ignored them. With slow deliberation he aroused her body to higher and higher levels of sensations, building a crescendo of feeling which pushed past barrier after barrier until Peggy pulsed with a molten yearning which was more pain than pleasure.

His name burst from her throat, a raw, primitive, mating call. And he answered it, soothing the frenzied edge of need as his flesh merged with hers, filling the throbbing emptiness with the ultimate satisfaction, then asserting their exquisite union with the age-old rhythm of possession. Together, and as one, their bodies played out the exultant tune of belonging, soaring up through octaves of pleasure to an ecstatic climax which sighed through them, completing all that had to be completed. Then they lay in blissful peace, entwined in each other's arms, their stillness imbued with utter contentment.

After a long, long silence, Adam's fingers feathered up her spine and entwined themselves in her curls. 'Do you hurt, Peggy?' he murmured caringly.

'No,' she whispered. He pressed his lips to her forehead.

'I want to thank you.'

She snuggled closer, a sweet smile of satisfaction curving her mouth. 'I should be thanking you. What do you want to thank me for?'

He sighed. 'I don't know—the gift of yourself. Making this night more special than any other night of my life.' The hand in her curls curved around her head, tucking it possessively under his chin. 'When I saw you in the theatre I felt relief. Then at interval . . . a tremendous buzz of anticipation. Afterwards in the car . . . excitement, frustration. But nothing . . . nothing I've ever felt before was like this.' He began stroking her hair. 'Tired?'

'Mmm . . . happy tired,' she mumbled, hugging his words to her heart.

'Me too.' He heaved another sigh and settled them both more comfortably, his body curved to hers. A hand slid around her waist and moved up to gently cup her breast. It was not an overture for more love-making, but a tender remembrance of what they had shared, almost an idle gesture but one which carried the need to have their sense of togetherness prolonged even into sleep.

Peggy smiled to herself. She had been special to him all along, even more so now. And it was the man whose hand lay tenderly over her heart, not the pop-star. A man who wanted her more than he had wanted any other woman, and she would fight to keep the man and make him hers. She knew the fight was worthwhile now.

CHAPTER TEN

ADAM was still sleeping peacefully. Peggy was loath to interrupt what was surely a much-needed rest but she could not go without some word to him. She would have hated to wake up alone after what they had shared last night. He looked curiously vulnerable with his body completely relaxed, and his unlined face seemed much younger than his twenty eight years. Peggy leaned over and lightly brushed the tousled hair from his forehead.

'Adam . . .' she called softly.

The thick black eyelashes flicked open instantly. For a moment his stare was blank and then puzzlement creased a frown. 'Why are you dressed?'

'I have to leave now. I just wanted to let you know.'

'Why?' He caught her hand and pulled her on to the bed. 'I want you to stay here with me, Peggy.' He was up on his elbow, the blue eyes fully alert and demanding her acquiescence.

Peggy sat next to him, her hand imprisoned by his, and the temptation was harder to fight with the remembrance of their intimacy throbbing between them. She would like nothing better than to push aside everything else and luxuriate in the pleasure of being with Adam. But common sense had argued against it. And won.

There was a time to play and a time to work. One of her assignments was due to be handed back today, and another handed out. If she did not go to the Institute she would miss important information and with the final examinations looming close, this was no time to be wagging lectures.

'I have a nine o'clock lecture, Adam,' she said apologetically. 'I must get home, change my clothes, and collect the books I need for today.'

'Don't go. It won't matter if you skip a lecture for once, will it?'

She sighed and cast him a wry smile. 'It's not just one. There are four I have to attend.'

'So? Copy up Gavin's notes on them. I'm sure he'd oblige you. Particularly after the capital he made out of last night,' he added cynically. He flopped back on to the pillow, pulling Peggy down to lie on his chest. His eyes held hers with a gleaming reminder of what they had shared, and his voice purred out soft persuasion.

'Spend the day with me, Peggy.' She almost gave in. Her heart clamoured to stay with him, but her mind gnawed over his casual dismissal of her work. She wanted to share his life, but not at the cost of her own. There had to be give and take from both sides for their relationship to be ultimately successful.

She touched his mouth with her finger tips, reinforcing the memory of last night's intimacy as her eyes challenged his. 'Would you give up your performance tonight if I asked you to stay with me?'

He jerked his head aside in impatient dismissal. 'You know that's not possible.'

Her eyebrows rose above eyes which hardened with stubborn purpose. 'Don't you have an understudy? Someone like Gavin who can go through the motions for you?'

He stared at her for a long moment, frowning his displeasure. 'The situations aren't comparable, Peggy,' he said with a touch of cold arrogance.

Inwardly she bristled but she managed to keep her voice calm. 'You mean your work is too important to toss aside, but mine can be brushed off whenever it interferes with what you want to do.'

He exploded with annoyance. 'No, dammit! I don't mean that. Stop putting words into my mouth.'

She pulled away from him and stood up. 'Then what do you mean, Adam?'

'For God's sake! We had something great last night! Is it so unreasonable that I should want it to continue today?'

'No. I'd like that too.'

'Well?'

'I'm not free today, just like you're not free tonight,' she repeated flatly.

His lips thinned into an exasperated grimace. 'Why are you fighting me? Dammit, Peggy! We could be making love right now.'

She sucked in a sharp breath. Her stomach was churning with the conflict of wanting him, yet being unable to accept his terms. 'I'm more than a body, Adam, and there's more to my life than making love. I won't sacrifice everything else for your pleasure.'

'And yours,' he reminded her savagely.

'Yes, mine,' she agreed, hating the whole argument but driven by her own sense of identity to continue it. She had had a taste of being Adam's consort last night and knew she would never be content with that role. She tried once more to explain her position.

'I could ask Gavin for his notes. At the price of a few snide cracks at the reason for my absence, I daresay he would oblige me. But I don't think he'd keep obliging me the next time and the next time. He and I are competing for the top place in our course, and our final examinations are coming up soon. I haven't come this far to throw away my chances now. You'd better understand that, Adam.'

'It's just one day!' he snapped in angry frustration.

Peggy's control broke against his refusal to consider her point of view. 'No, it's not! It's your whole self-centred attitude,' she retorted fiercely. 'You want what you want when you want it, like the party last night. You had a marvellous time playing the great Adam Gale to all your admirers, and it was only when you were finished with them that you turned to me. You want me at your convenience, and it's your convenience to have me today. So to hell with what I should be doing!'

The blue eyes held no desire now, no softness. They were diamond-hard. 'Well, I'm sorry it's not your convenience to stay with me,' he said sarcastically. 'Obviously your work comes ahead of anything we might have. I wish you a happy day.'

Peggy stared at him, the chill of his dismissal freezing her blood. She couldn't let it end here, not

after last night. She had to reach him. She had to.
She moistened her lips and forced her voice to calm
reason. 'I respect your need and your right to work
as you see fit, Adam. I wouldn't ask you to give it up
for me, not one minute of it. All I'm asking is that
you give the same respect to my work. It may not
seem very important to you but it's important to
me.'

'I can see that,' he bit out acidly.

Tears pricked at her eyes. It was obvious from his
intractable mood that any more words would be
futile and pride forced Peggy to turn and walk
away. Her heart screamed for Adam to say
something . . . anything . . . as her feet took her to
the spiral staircase and plodded reluctantly down
the steps. But the silence behind her was absolute.

Her shoulders slumped in defeat as she reached
the lower floor. She stood there, her hand still on the
banister, a turmoil of emotion clouding the judgement she had made. She desperately wanted to go
back to him, to hang on to what had begun last
night, whatever the cost.

But the sickening truth could not be dismissed. It
was too late to change her mind; the damage had
been done. She could not go back upstairs and
recapture the togetherness of last night. And her
mind insisted that Adam had to recognise the
realities in her words or there was nowhere for their
relationship to go beyond bed. And as satisfying as
that had been, Peggy knew instinctively that it
would not satisfy for long if it was not backed up by
an understanding of other needs.

With a heavy heart, she left the hotel and

ravelled home. Adam did not follow her. She went
o the Institute and attended her lectures. She
eceived a High Distinction for her assignment but
t gave her no pleasure. Her concentration was shot
o pieces. She took notes haphazardly and the only
hing she really got straight was the subject of her
lext assignment.

Gavin was cock-a-hoop over the contacts he had
nade at the party, but Peggy very curtly shut him up
when he attempted a probe on her relationship with
Adam. That was far too painful a point to allow
even the slightest rub, and she didn't care what
Gavin thought, as long as he kept his thoughts to
limself.

The last lecture ended at four o'clock. Peggy
walked straight out of the Institute and on to a bus
or Circular Quay. The ferry ride across the harbour
lid not evoke any interest today. Peggy's eyes were
urned inward, seeing Adam in her mind, running
hrough the whole range of her experience with
lim.

She wished she had played this morning's scene
lifferently. Confrontation was hardly the weapon
of persuasion! The issue could have been postponed
o a more receptive time instead of her hitting
Adam with it virtually upon his waking. She had
oeen a fool, a proud, stubborn fool. For all the work
she had done today, she might as well have been
with Adam, and she would have been a great deal
lappier.

The ferry reached the Neutral Bay wharf and
Peggy disembarked, feeling totally miserable with
lerself and her world. She trudged up the hill

towards her apartment block, her bag of book
growing heavier, along with her heart. She took no
notice of the footsteps coming towards her, she
didn't even glance up until a hand took the bag from
her grasp. Startled, she had already opened her
mouth to cry a protest when her eyes swept up to the
face which had been in her thoughts all day.

'Adam,' she breathed in a dizzying rush of relief,
then flung her arms around his neck in uninhibited
delight. He dropped her bag and hugged her to him,
laughing in his own relief at her impulsive greeting.
'Does this mean I'm welcome?'

'Oh, Adam! I was so stupid this morning,
standing on my high-horse and shooting my mouth
off. And you had every right to expect . . .'

He placed a finger on her lips, hushing her
babble. The blue eyes held apology as he spoke.
'No, you were right, Peggy, and I was wrong. I've
had the whole day to think about it, and the truth is
I have become used to women who've gone along
with whatever I wanted. I should've known you'd
be different.' He suddenly grinned at her and lifted
his hand to rub the cheek she had slapped after the
Ross Elliot Show. 'You did warn me.'

She grinned back at him, deliriously happy that
he had accepted the stand she had taken and was
here, wanting to be with her. 'I would have loved
spending the day with you, Adam. I hated having to
go.'

'Well, we've got a couple of hours now before I
have to go,' he said with dry irony. 'I bought some
Chinese takeaway in the hope that you would share
it with me.'

'That's great!' she beamed. 'I haven't eaten a thing all day and I'm starving.'

Adam laughed and picked up her bag. His free hand curled possessively around hers. Peggy's feet felt as light as air as they climbed up the rest of the hill with Adam alongside her. They collected the food from the Range Rover and at Adam's urging, Peggy told him all about her day at the Institute.

Once inside her bedsitter he did not make love to her as she had half-expected, half-wanted. Instead he drew her out about her course, showing a keen interest in what she was studying. They chatted on about the communications field, and since Adam knew the many angles of filming from having made dozens of videos for his songs, Peggy soon forgot about lovemaking in the exhilaration of talking about her favourite subject.

She heated up the Chinese food, and it was the most enjoyable meal Peggy had ever had. Not only did it satisfy her physical hunger, but Adam's company was satisfying the hunger in her to share all her ideas with him. He sat across the table from her and there was no communication gap at all; no awkward silences, no struggle for understanding. They bounced ideas off each other, matched wits, exchanged some of the more memorable moments in their lives; and all the time their eyes sparkled with pleasure.

'I'll have to leave now,' Adam finally said on a reluctant sigh. His eyes were suddenly serious, projecting a sharp intensity of feeling. 'I'd like to come back here after the show.'

He was not presuming her acquiescence as he had

presumed it last night, and Peggy was deeply moved by the respect he was giving to her wishes. 'I'd like that too,' she answered without hesitation, her eyes assuring him he was more than welcome.

He rose from the table, smiling with happy anticipation. 'I could make it back by eleven-thirty.'

'I haven't any champagne,' she warned as he lifted her into his embrace.

'With you I don't need it,' he declared very positively, and kissed her with a fervour which was more intoxicating than any wine.

Peggy responded with all the choked feeling that had been building up all day, her whole body pressing her need for him.

Adam heaved a ragged sigh and his eyes mirrored the same urgent desire that was racing through Peggy's veins. 'Tonight,' he promised, and planted a firm farewell kiss on her forehead.

Peggy closed the door after him and leaned against it, hugging herself from sheer happiness. She was deeply, wildly in love with Adam Gale and nothing would ever be the same again. Now that the misery of the day was in the past, she exulted over the results of her fight with Adam this morning. There could not be any doubt now that she really was special to him. Whatever pattern Adam had followed with his previous love affairs, this one was going to be different! She would make it different. She wanted this love affair to last for ever.

She danced around her small apartment, tidying it up, dusting, putting fresh sheets on her bed. She had a shower, washed her hair, then listened to

Adam's tape of *Blind Date* as she gave herself a manicure and a pedicure and carefully varnished both sets of nails. By eleven-thirty she was tingling with anticipation.

The clock moved on. Eleven-forty-five. So he was a bit late. Maybe he had been caught up with fans after the show? He would get away as soon as he could. She just had to be patient. Adam was a star and fans could be very demanding of a star.

Midnight. Peggy's ears strained to hear a footfall in the stairwell. Surely any minute now.

Twelve-thirty. She paced the floor of her living-room, fear fighting with anger. Something had happened to him. No, nothing had happened to him. He was having a great time, not even noticing how late it was. After all, Peggy wasn't going to go away. She was at home, waiting up for him, waiting to give him what he wanted. When he got around to wanting it.

Twelve-forty-five. Peggy snapped off the lights and flounced into bed. He could have telephoned! The least he could have done was let her know he was delayed. But no. He hadn't thought of her. Well, damn him to hell! He could have his rotten pop-star life to himself. Tears trickled out of the corners of her eyes. How could he do this to her after all their talking? And kissing her as though he could barely tear himself away.

The doorbell rang and Peggy's heart jumped, but pride made her stay in bed. Pride said he could ring all night and she wouldn't answer him. The doorbell rang again, more insistently. Anger whispered that she should give him a piece of her mind, a damned

good piece of her mind. She flung the bedclothes off
and stamped out to the door.

He stood there, apology in his eyes but lipstick on
his face! Lipstick!

'I'm sorry for being so . . .'

She exploded. 'How dare you think you can come
home to me with another woman's lipstick on your
face!'

'Lipstick?'

His frowning question infuriated her. She
stepped back to slam the door in his face but he
thrust out an arm, halting the action.

'Go away!' she shrilled. 'Go back to where you've
been. Go to hell for all I care!'

He pushed inside and shut the door, pulling her
into his arms at the same time and holding her tight
to quell her resistance. 'I can explain, Peggy. I'm
sorry I'm late, and I'm sorry you're upset. But I can
explain if you'll listen.'

She glared at him, fire and brimstone in her eyes,
but already the physical magic he could exert was
working on her defiant resistance.

'My father came to visit me after the show
tonight. My *father*, Peggy. And his new wife, who
kissed me goodbye when I left them. I came home to
you as soon as I decently could.'

His father! His father from whom he had been
estranged for so many years. Her anger was
instantly wiped out. 'Oh, Adam! That's marvellous,' she breathed in sympathetic happiness for
him.

'Well, I can tell you it was a shock.' His face
relaxed into a rueful smile. 'I was as awkward as a

boy. Can you believe that?'

She laughed and shook her head. 'Did he finally recognise your talent, Adam?'

He grinned. 'I suspect his wife has urged him on but yes, he was generous in his peace-making.'

'Oh, I'm so glad for you. And what about your brothers?'

'My stepmother is planning a family party when the show goes to Melbourne.'

'That's great! Isn't it great?' she added when Adam didn't answer her.

'You're some kind of girl, Peggy Dean,' he said huskily, his eyes glowing with tenderness and desire. 'I should have thought to call you. Forgive me?'

'Only this time,' she threatened, but her eyes were giving him another answer.

There was an extra exhilaration in their lovemaking, a greater depth of feeling in their mutual possession. The sensual magic of the previous night was woven again but with a more meaningful appreciation of each other. It was more than magic, it was real. And when they eventually fell asleep, their faces wore the beautiful peace of utter contentment.

Most of Saturday morning had passed before they stirred awake. Peggy lay in the curve of Adam's arm, her body pressed against his, and she had no desire to move at all. She decided that her weekly shopping could wait until Monday. Any necessary provisions could be bought at the corner shop this afternoon while Adam was doing his matinée show.

There was enough food in the refrigerator for lunch.

'I wish I didn't have to go this afternoon,' Adam murmured, his mood obviously matching hers. He heaved a sigh and turned towards her, his lips brushing across her temples. 'At least we'll have all day tomorrow to ourselves.'

A cold little chill ran down Peggy's spine. Adam had forgotten her Sunday job. She did not want to spoil this lovely mood of contentment but neither could she let him go on anticipating what would not come about. She sucked in a deep breath, savagely regretting the need for another confrontation about her work.

'I'm sorry, Adam, but we haven't got all day tomorrow. I did tell you I have a waitressing job on Sundays, and I can't not go. I need the money to live on. I explained that to you at Harry's Place.'

Silence. Stillness. She felt his breathing accelerate as if he was about to explode with frustration, but then it stilled also, as if his mind was working so furiously it had suspended all other bodily functions. In an abrupt move, Adam heaved himself up on his elbow and there was determined purpose in the eyes which now challenged her.

'This job is just for money—it's not important to you for any other reason?' he demanded more than asked.

'Adam, I can't make do without it,' she said in a tone of gentle appeasement.

'Well, that's easily disposed of. I'll give you the money and you can give up the job.'

The cold little chill instantly developed spikes of ice. She could not trust herself to speak. Some

orner of sanity told her that Adam was undoubted-
y accustomed to women who accepted whatever he
vas willing to give in the way of money or gifts but
t made no difference to the revulsion she felt at his
·ffer.

'I can't take money from you, Adam,' she stated
latly.

He frowned. 'Why not? It's no problem to me and
·ou can pay me back when you get the job you really
vant if you feel you have to. It's not as if this Sunday
vork is critical to your future career.'

Her dark eyes pleaded for understanding. 'I'd
ıate it, Adam, every time you gave me money. It'd
ıake me feel you were buying me.'

His mouth tightened. 'You know that leaves us
vith the frustration of only having snatches of time
ogether. With you working days and me nights . . .'
ıe shook his head in mute protest at the situation,
there's only Sunday.'

'I'm sorry, but the job is security to me, and jobs
ren't easy to get, Adam.' Peggy sighed despondent-
y. She hated the waitressing job more than ever.
Most Sundays she was run off her legs and only the
·ay cheque had kept her in it. Never in her life had
ıe wished so much that she received the parental
llowances that other students took for granted. It
vas poor comfort to tell herself that her parents had
ılways done their best by her and that up until today
ıe had been proud of being able to support herself.

'How much do you make?'

The blunt question raised her gaze to Adam's
·nce more. His frustration had been replaced with a
·ery intent look.

'Seventy dollars,' she answered dully.

'I have a cheque-book in the Range Rover. If I write you a cheque for two thousand dollars now that should cover all your living expenses until you've completed your course, shouldn't it?'

'Yes, but . . .'

'Please listen, Peggy. Consider it a loan which you can pay back when you're on your feet financially. You can put it in the bank on Monday and draw on it at your own convenience. No strings attached. Is that enough security for you?'

The appeal in his eyes and the tug of her own heart were too strong to resist. It was a way out of the impasse which erased most of her objections and she cut the last stubborn strand of pride. 'Yes,' she breathed in quick surrender. Then despite her decision, a flood of embarrassment swept colour into her cheeks. 'It's very generous of you, Adam. I promise you I'll pay back what I use.'

His face wore a triumphant grin as he jumped out of bed and started dragging on the tracksuit he had worn last night. 'Peggy, I wouldn't care if you never repaid a cent of it, so long as you're happy.'

He tossed her her dressing-gown. 'Come on, I want you to 'phone your ex-employer right now and I'll have that cheque in your hand before you've delivered your resignation from his staff. And don't forget to make that resignation immediate, right?'

'Right,' she agreed, feeling quite dizzy. Maybe Adam was still buying her in a way, but she did not care any more. For him to trust her with such a large sum of money had to mean that she meant a great deal to him, more than she had dared hope. She

would not need anywhere near that much to see her
through to the end of the academic year and of
course she would repay him what she did use, but
the most significant point of Adam's offer was that
he could not be anticipating an early end to their
affair.

She slipped her arms into her dressing-gown and
tied it around her. Adam steered her to the
telephone then left her to make the call. Peggy's
employer was annoyed at the late notice, but since
she had been hired on a casual basis he could not do
anything about it but grumble at her lack of
consideration. Peggy was regretful, polite, but firm,
and ended the call with the hollow feeling of having
burnt her bridges. She was still sitting on the sofa
beside the telephone when Adam returned and slid
his cheque under one corner of the handset.

She was unaware of the intense vulnerability in
her eyes as he took her hands and pulled her to her
feet. His arms slid around her waist, supporting her
in a gentle embrace as he spoke softly, caringly.
'Was it such a hard step to take, Peggy?'

She let out her tension in a sigh and put on a self-
mocking smile. 'I guess I've become used to being
independent. It's a bit scary giving that up, Adam.'

'Doesn't the cheque give you independence?'

'Yes. Yes, of course it does. And I do want the
time free to spend with you,' she assured him
warmly.

'I've just been thinking about that.' The blue eyes
searched hers, probing carefully. 'Would you
consider moving in with me?'

The suggestion stopped her heart altogether for a

moment. Then it beat a painful tattoo against the tight constriction of her chest. Living together! That's what he meant. The idea was both exciting and alarming. Her mind whirled with it. To be with Adam every available moment, day after day. There was no doubt that she wanted that, but was it the right move ... what would she be to him?

Would it reduce her to the same category as the other women he had had live with him ... the ones she had idly read about in magazines ... those who had been there before her and passed out of his life? She did not want to become a convenience, a fixture he took for granted instead of a woman he valued.

And her parents would die if the fact were ever publicised. At least her mother would. But Adam had promised he would protect her from publicity. Maybe she would escape media notice for long enough to entrench herself in Adam's life. A permanent fixture.

'If your independence means so much to you, there's no reason you can't keep paying rent on this flat,' Adam argued reasonably, then deepened his tone to soft persuasion. 'But I want to come home to you every night, Peggy.'

And she wanted that too. Every night. Always. And Adam might get addicted to the emotional security she could give him, enough to want it always. 'In for a penny, in for a pound' ... the phrase flitted through her mind and was instantly rejected. This was no 'pound'. It was the whole treasure chest of her life she would be giving him, and if he spent it carelessly she would curl up and die.

But she wouldn't let him do that, her strong, inner voice insisted. Hadn't she always fought for what she wanted? And got it most of the time. 'Anything worth having is worth fighting for,' Edward Knight had said, and Peggy believed it. She would be on Adam's home ground, given free rein on his territory, right at the heart of him.

She slid her hands up over his broad shoulders, and linked them behind his neck, her eyes clinging to the desire in his. 'Yes,' she whispered huskily.

'Does that mean yes, you will consider it, or yes, you will move in with me?' Adam asked, a husky note roughening his voice.

A smile tugged at her mouth; she could see that it really mattered to him. A matter of considerable importance. 'I'll move in with you, Adam.'

He breathed a sigh of palpable relief and his smile sparkled into his eyes, making them more vividly blue than ever. 'I could come back here tonight and help you pack your things tomorrow,' he said eagerly.

'All right,' she agreed.

With a whoop of unbridled delight Adam lifted her up in the air and swung her around. She landed back against his body, breathless and flustered, and allowed no time to recover. Adam's mouth devoured hers in a kiss which set her heart hammering and her bones melting and her mind spinning into splattered chaos.

'You know what I like most about you, Peggy?' Adam grinned at her while she was still struggling to put herself back to order.

'What?' The automatic response.

His grin widened. 'The way you come straight out with what you think. No beating around the bush with Peggy Dean, no sir. You play it right off the top.'

Only I'm not playing, Peggy thought ruefully. This is no game to me. And if you think it is, Adam Gale, then I'll teach you different, right off the top. With love.

CHAPTER ELEVEN

'PEGGY!' She smiled to herself, her heart automatically lifting at Adam's call. Every night he came bursting into the house, shouting her name as if he couldn't wait to be with her.

'I'm in the lounge,' she called back, putting her book down and pushing herself out of the armchair in her own eagerness to greet him. It would be a fortnight tomorrow since she had come to live with Adam and the magic of his presence had not dimmed in the slightest degree.

He came striding into the room, his face alight with triumph. 'I've got it! I've really got it this time! It came to me on the way home. Come up to the music-room with me and I'll play it for you and you can tell me if I'm right.' He grabbed her hand and literally hauled her after him as he bounded up the stairs. 'Now sit there and listen,' he commanded, pushing her into a chair.

Peggy sat at attention, slightly bemused by Adam's valuing her opinion so much. While she loved music, she was hardly an expert on its technicalities. All week Adam had been working on this new song while she had attended her lectures at The Institute. The tune had sounded good to her but he had insisted it was not quite right. He had tried different variations, all of which had only caused him more niggling frustration. Now, as he seated himself at his electronic keyboard, he was exuding confidence, and she felt ridiculously happy for him.

Heightening her pleasure was the fact that she had actually helped Adam with the lyrics. He had been browsing through her text-book for Social History when he came up with the idea of writing a satirical song on the euphemisms used by politicians when commenting on events. The concept had become even more exciting when Adam had enthused over her ideas for the video of the song.

Adam ran through the opening chords. His vivid blue eyes sparkled at her as he began singing their words, then dropped to the keyboard as he concentrated on the new notes to be played. She recognised the different phrasing immediately and knew Adam was right. It gave the tune more bite, a sharper dramatic edge which carried precisely the impact the song needed. She clapped her hands and dashed across the room to hug him with delight.

'Yes, yes, yes! You're a genius, Adam,' she bubbled in his ear.

He laughed and pulled her down on to his lap. 'And you know what else I thought? Why don't you direct the video for me, Peggy? The song can wait until you finish your course.'

Excitement welled up: and shone out of her eyes. 'Oh, Adam! I'd love to. But I'd have to get into the business first and I don't know . . .'

He placed a hushing finger on her lips and his grin was deliciously smug. 'I thought of that too. Since we're going to the Knights' for lunch tomorrow, we can talk it over with Robert and ask him how it can be organised. I want you to do it,

Peggy. I want to have your vision of it.'

The words were teetering on her tongue again, bursting to be spoken, and she kissed him fast to prevent them from tumbling out. 'I love you, I love you,' her heart pounded as Adam's hand slid over it, moving to caress the soft fullness of her breasts. She felt him grow hard with desire for her and her own desire for him was as strong as it had ever been, but as each day had passed, Peggy's craving for emotional security had grown even stronger. It wasn't enough that he wanted her. She wanted to hear him say he loved her ... loved her as he had loved no other woman ... exclusively, rapturously, and for ever after.

But not once had he spoken of love, and Peggy was too proud to beg for it. She knew that to say the words herself would be an automatic request that they be returned, so she had kept them locked inside, waiting and hoping. She and Adam were closer at this moment than at any time before, exulting in the shared creation of their minds as well as feeling the same sexual chemistry, and she willed him to speak with all her being.

He made love to her. His mouth and his hands and his whole body were expertly eloquent at making love. He carried Peggy into the bedroom and very slowly and with exquisite sensitivity, brought her to a new peak of physical ecstasy. Afterwards he gently caressed and cradled her into a peaceful languor. Then he spoke. He talked about Jenny Ross and Robert Knight and how Robert had promoted her songs, and eventually his words slurred with weariness and he drifted off to sleep.

Peggy lay awake in the darkness and not even the warmth of Adam's body could prevent a cold wave of loneliness from creeping into her heart. Tears pricked her eyes and gathered in their corners. A welling trickle coursed down her cheeks and dampened the curls near her ears. She had seen the love between Jenny and her husband and as Adam had spoken of them, she had hoped he would liken their own relationship to Jenny's and Robert's, but he had not made that connection.

She had done all she could to make it happen. She had taught him to share, sometimes subtly, more often with blunt confrontation to which Adam had always responded, although not without some argument. Their first week together had been a little rocky, but this last week had held pure touches of heaven. If only Adam would say he loved her, Peggy could rest content. But he had not said it, and she suspected that if he could not say it now, he never would. The black clouds of depression rolled over her mind and the tears fell faster. Peggy turned her face into the pillow and silently cried herself to sleep.

Sunday brought a beautiful spring morning; a flood of friendly sunshine, blue skies, not even a nip in the air as Peggy and Adam set up breakfast on the patio. Peggy loved Adam's home. It was modern and comfortable with lovely, big, spacious rooms which he had furnished more to his pleasure than in any particular style. On the patio around the swimming-pool was a large aluminium lace table where they sat with the Sunday newspapers spread around their breakfast.

They ate their peaches and muesli, pausing to read out snippets of news to each other, as comfortable together as any old married couple. Only they were not married, and Peggy doubted that Adam had marriage on his mind. She sighed away the lurking tentacles of last night's depression and turned another page of her newspaper.

Her own face jumped out at her—a blow-up from the accompanying photograph of her and Adam arriving at the Hilton Hotel. The caption sent a shot of horror up her spine.

ADAM GALE'S NEW LIVE-IN LADY BLIND DATE STRIKES JACKPOT AT THEATRE AND HOME

Her stunned gaze ran through the story below. In the most titillating style of gossip journalism, her meeting with Adam on the Ross Elliot Show was recounted, her appearance with him at the première party and Adam's insistence on the word, 'lady', were highlighted with suggestive glee, and then the damning information that she was living in Adam's house was detailed in undeniable facts.

Peggy felt sick. Right there in indelible print was her private and personal affair, laid bare for a sniggering public, a cheap thrill for readers. And no one would give a damn what she felt. The article was full of sexual implications but did not bother to suggest that an emotional tie might exist between her and Adam. She was simply the latest in a line of live-in ladies who were named and their time with Adam briefly documented.

'Listen to this . . .' Adam glanced up and noticed her frozen pallor. 'What's wrong?'

She passed him the page without a word; her hand was trembling as she withdrew it. She clenched it into a tight, steady fist and watched Adam's face with unwavering concentration, knowing his reaction would be important to her—critical as far as their relationship was concerned.

He frowned as he read. His mouth curled with distaste. 'Sleazy bastard,' he muttered, then tossed the page away in disgust. 'God! What they'll do for a story! Ignore it, Peggy. The only way to treat this kind of gutter press is simply to deny its existence.'

Her heart stopped fluttering. Everything within her was still ... waiting ... as she trod the last tightrope towards Adam's heart. 'But it does exist, Adam. Other people are reading it right now,' she said very quietly and very calmly.

He grimaced in exasperation and made a sharp dismissive gesture. 'So what does it matter what they think? Little people ... little minds,' he muttered contemptuously.

'My mother and father will be reading it.'

He shook his head as if the whole matter had nuisance value only ... something to be shrugged off, of no real account. He caught Peggy's steely look and frowned at her. 'What do you want me to say? I'm sorry?'

She said nothing. His tone of voice had been one of irritation, as if he thought she was making a mountain out of a molehill.

He threw up his hands in mock surrender. 'Okay, I'm sorry! But you knew I drew this kind of publicity, Peggy. Much as I deplore it and try to avoid it, there's not a lot I can do to prevent it.

You've just got to shrug it off if you're associated with me.'

'Yes, I guess I do,' she said sadly, forced now to face up to the truth that she was not uniquely special to Adam. Just the latest in a line of live-in ladies. She had failed. A wave of nausea kept Peggy seated a moment longer and then she forced herself to her feet. 'Please give my apology to the Knights, Adam, I can't go to their lunch with you. I have to go home.'

'What?' It was a bark of incredulity.

Peggy had already turned away, heading for the glass doors into the sunroom, and she did not turn back. 'Just tell them I had to go home. I'm sure they'll understand,' she said in a flat, toneless voice.

'What do you mean . . . you have to go home?' Adam demanded truculently.

Peggy sucked in a deep breath and exerted the utmost control over her emotions. She half-turned, her whole bearing one of stiff dignity. Her eyes were cold and proud and very, very distant, and her voice seemed to come from some dim, hollow place.

'My parents have always been very proud of me, Adam. I didn't tell them about moving in with you because it's not the kind of behaviour they expect of me. It's not the kind of behaviour I ever expected of myself, but I did it. I can bear the consequences of my actions but it's not only I who's hurt by that story. My mother will be devastated by it, my father shocked, and I think, disappointed in me. The only thing I can do to alleviate the hurt I've given them is to go home and try to explain why I . . .' tears pricked her eyes and she swallowed hard to prevent

any wobble to her voice, 'why I let them down. I jus
hope I'll be able to make them understand. Pleas
excuse me.'

She fled up to the bedroom and hastily shoved a
few things into a bag. She darted into the en-suite
bathroom for her comb and toothbrush and
returned to find Adam in the bedroom doorway, hi
expression set in an odd mixture of frustration and
concern.

'Don't you think you're over-reacting?' he ac
cused gruffly, then cleared his throat. 'It's no grea
scandal these days for a couple to be found living
together. Your parents must have friends whose
kids are doing the same thing.'

It was an effort to speak, even more of an effort to
speak calmly. But she managed it, controlling the
turmoil of pain and despair which wanted to cry ou
and rail at him. It had been her gamble, and it was
not his fault that her judgement had been wrong
'My parents are old, Adam, and my mother, in
particular, has a very old-fashioned view of moral
ity. And what other people's daughters do would be
no excuse for her daughter.'

'What does she live in? The Victorian Age?' he
snapped.

Peggy clamped her mouth shut and zipped up her
bag. There was no point in saying any more. At this
moment she and Adam were almost strangers. She
looked at him and saw a very handsome man, but
the desire which had bound her to him ever since
they had met, was now ashes in her heart.

Maybe he too felt the sudden distance between
them for he stepped forward, hands lifting in a

gesture of appeasement. 'Peggy . . .'

She cut him off. 'I don't want to argue with you, Adam. I'm leaving now to catch the first available train to Wyong.'

He jerked his head in an impatient negative. 'Can't you telephone your parents? Go this afternoon if you feel you have to. Damn it, Peggy! You're entitled to live your own life. We were going to talk to Robert about the song. Surely to God . . .'

The song! Their song! The pain of loss ripped through Peggy's heart, then ruthless logic blocked it out. Whether she was here or not, Adam would go on creating music. It was *his* song. Adam was still talking, arguing his case . . . his desires . . . his convenience.

She broke into his speech, sharply and decisively. 'You can talk to Robert, Adam, you don't really need me. Now please, I must be going.'

He sighed, his eyes raking her with ill-humour. 'You're getting this all out of proportion, Peggy.'

'Maybe I've just found a new perspective,' she retorted with savage irony. 'Goodbye, Adam.'

She brushed by him but he caught her hand, forcing a halt. His eyes stabbed angrily at her. 'There's no cause for you to take that tone with me. I'll drive you in to Central Station if you're so bloody intent on going.'

'Thank you, I'd appreciate that,' she replied, cool politeness deflecting his anger.

The traffic was light and the trip to Central from Adam's home in Mosman only took twenty minutes. Twenty minutes of heavy silence. Peggy had no more to say and Adam was obviously not going

to beg her to stay, not that his begging would change
her mind. If Adam had loved her, he would have
wanted to go with her ... stand by her ... do
whatever he could to ease the situation.

He accompanied her to the station office, waited
by her as she bought the ticket, and walked her to
the designated platform. Tension walked with them
every step of the way, the screaming tension of
unspoken words which were pleading to be said. It
was a tortured relief to Peggy when they reached the
ticket-barrier. The train was waiting. It was due to
leave in ten minutes. She looked up at Adam with
carefully expressionless eyes.

'Thank you,' she said, louder than she had meant
to. *Thank you, farewell, God be with you, my love*, her
heart cried.

His face was set in stiff, proud lines. 'When will
you be back?'

'I don't know,' she murmured and turned away.

A hand grasped her shoulder, fingers digging
hard into her flesh. 'What do you mean ... you
don't know?' Harsh, grated words.

She sighed to relieve the painful constriction in
her chest and shook her head without looking back
at him. 'I just don't know, Adam. Please let me go.
You're hurting me.'

He let her go and she walked briskly down the
platform, fighting to hold back tears. She had not
meant to look back. With one foot already on the
train, she was about to step into the carriage when
some inner compulsion dragged her gaze back to
where he had been.

He had not moved. He stood where she had left

im . . . tall, straight, so still he could almost have
een a statue, his gaze locked on to hers. He did not
aise a hand in farewell. They stared at each other
cross a distance which could still have been
ridged . . . if he really cared for her. If he had
eached out . . . called her name . . . come after her
. . but he made no move.

Peggy wrenched her gaze away. She stepped on to
ie train, blundered past the inner door and sank
ito the first available window seat, blinking
iriously. Her heart was hammering a protest at the
ictates of her mind but she sat on through the long,
readful minutes while the train waited on its
eparture time. Every fibre of her being was
oncentrated on willing Adam to come to her.
Vhen the train finally lurched into motion she
igged back in her seat, defeat dragging her into
ull listlessness.

She watched the suburbs roll by with blank,
mpty eyes, and after a while she didn't really see
nything. A vast greyness filled her soul and her
iind automatically rejected the torment of thought.
he train terminated at Wyong, which was fortu-
ate, for only when the carriage had emptied did
eggy realise she had reached her destination.

She trudged home, relieved not to meet anyone
ie had to acknowledge on the way. She mentally
raced herself as she walked up the front path of her
arents' modest little home. It was her father who
nswered the doorbell, a sure sign that all was not
ell inside.

'Hello, Dad,' she said on a rueful sigh, then had to
ite her lips to stop them trembling. 'I guess you

know why I'm here.'

His eyes questioned her, a ready compassion softening the pain. 'He's not with you?'

A huge lump gorged her throat. She shook her head, unable to speak.

His sigh was very heavy. 'It's not a good day, Peggy, but I'm glad you came home.' He put a comforting arm around her shoulders and drew her inside. 'Your mother's taking it hard.'

Somehow Peggy dredged up the inner strength to bear her mother's tearful reproaches. She was intensely grateful to her father for his kind mediation in lessening the stress of the situation. He did not condemn or excuse, but gently soothed the hurts on both sides until there was an uneasy peace in the house. Peggy was forgiven the scandal she had brought upon them but it was not forgotten . . would not be forgotten for many a long day.

By late afternoon she felt utterly drained and more wretched than she had ever felt in her life. Her father invited her to join him as he watered the garden which was his pride and joy, second to her . . . at least it had been second to her, she thought miserable with guilt. It was a beautiful garden resplendent now with sweet peas, stocks, Iceland poppies and pansies, and her father played the hose gently over his beloved flowers. The beauty around her dimmed Peggy's troubles for a few moments . . until her father spoke.

'Are you going back to him, Peggy?'

She glanced sharply at her father, saw only concern for her in his eyes and looked away. 'I don't know what to do,' she mumbled, then in defiant elf-defence she blurted out, 'I love him, Dad.'

He cast her a sad, little smile. 'I didn't think nything else.' He drew in a deep breath and softly ut pointedly added, 'He should have come with ou today, Peggy.'

Her eyes met his unflinchingly, acknowledging he truth which she had already faced . . . faced, but till fought against accepting. 'He . . . he might earn to love me, Dad.'

Her father slowly shook his head. 'He should ave come with you.'

'Peggy . . .' her mother called from the back orch, '. . . you're wanted on the 'phone. It's him,' he added with tight resentment.

Adam? Calling her here? With a little hope ghtening the weight in her heart, she sped inside, nd then was almost too frightened to pick up the eceiver. A tumult of emotion churned through her s she paused, then in a spurt of self-determination he snatched up the instrument and spoke.

'Hello . . .'

'Peggy?'

Even the sound of Adam's voice weakened any esolve 'Yes it's me ' she affirmed shakily.

'Peggy, I want you to marry me'.

CHAPTER TWELVE

I *WANT you to marry me*. Peggy could hardly believe her ears. Just like that. Over the telephone. *I want you to marry me*. Blunt. Firm. Decisive. No question about it. *I want you to marry me*. Elation burst through her veins and danced like sparkling fire wheels through her brain.

'Peggy?' The slight hint of uncertainty in his voice prompted an immediate answer.

'Yes.' The word whooshed out on a high tide of wonderful feeling. 'I'll marry you. If you want me to,' she gabbled breathlessly.

'That's fine! That's great!' The words sounded like an explosion of feeling from his end too. 'Now give me directions and I'll drive up there, meet your parents, set their minds at rest, and bring you back home. All right?'

'All right!' It was difficult to form words. She was grinning from ear to ear. Somehow she managed to give him coherent directions.

'I'll be there in an hour or so. And Peggy . . .' his voice softened, 'I'm sorry about today. It won't happen again. I promised to protect you all I could and by God, I will! We'll get married as fast as can be arranged and everyone's going to know you're my wife, not some temporary girlfriend. So you tell your parents that. Okay?'

'Yes, Adam. Thank you,' she murmured huskily.

180

another wave of emotion hit her.

'Be with you soon. Don't go away,' Adam
commanded, then cut the connection.

Tears of relief and happiness coursed down
Peggy's cheeks. Adam had not said he loved her but
he cared enough to want to protect her. And they
would be married. Surely that meant he wanted a
lasting relationship? A permanent relationship?

'Peggy?'

Her father had come in. She turned towards him,
a watery smile wobbling assurance that everything
was all right. 'He's coming, Dad. He wants to marry
me.' She flew into the arms which had always held
out comfort to her and she gave her father a tight
hug, a hug of gratitude and triumph.

'Well now, I reckon thats something your mother
would like to hear,' he declared warmly and steered
her into the kitchen.

Marjorie Dean was struck dumb. All afternoon
she had rained words on Peggy's head, but now her
mouth opened and shut without one word coming
out. But she recovered fast and her face relaxed into
righteous satisfaction. 'Well, so he should. So he
would, was the starting chorus, but the tune grew
more and more cheerful as she fussed about what
Adam might like for dinner since he would be
arriving right on meal-time.

When the doorbell finally rang Peggy raced to
answer it. An uncharacteristic moment of shyness
held her back from flinging herself at Adam. He
had no such hesitation. He almost swept her off her
feet as he clutched her to him and the breath which

whistled past Peggy's ear sounded like blissfu
relief.

'No more walking away from me, Peggy Dear
you hear?' he commanded with considerable force
then kissed her with a passion which reinforced th
command very satisfactorily.

For the next two hours Adam delighted Pegg
with the way he worked hard at winning over he
parents, assuring them that he sincerely wanted t
share the best of all possible futures with thei
daughter, and would announce that, very publicly
thereby killing any stories to the contrary. Marjori
Dean fell an easy victim to his persuasive charm
such was the power Adam would always have ove
women, Peggy thought ruefully, but then wa
reminded of her own power over him. He had com
to her, and even her father looked content as sh
and Adam took their leave to go back to Sydney

Adam drove the Range Rover around the firs
corner, then pulled it over to the kerb.

'What's the matter?' Peggy asked in surprise.

'Something I want to say,' he murmured, switch
ing off the ignition. He turned to her and took he
hand in his, fondling it as if it were infinitel
precious. There was a new tenderness in the eye
which were appealing softly to her. 'I didn
understand what you were feeling this mornin
Peggy. To me it was just another Adam Gale stor
which specialised in half-truths. It seemed that yo
were putting your parents' feelings ahead of wha
we had together, and I resented your droppin
everything to go to them. Then when you walke
away from me . . . stepped on to that train . . . I g

is awful feeling that you were walking out of my
e. I couldn't shake it. I had to fight the urge to go
1d haul you out of that train.'

He sighed and gave her a rueful little smile. 'Pride
opped me. I went off to our luncheon date with the
nights, angry because I had to apologise for your
osence. But they *did* understand, Peggy, and their
w comments jolted me into seeing the whole thing
fferently. Then after lunch Edward challenged
e to a game of chess and we went into his study. I
ouldn't concentrate, I kept thinking of you. He
rought up the party at the Hilton and mentioned
ow much he'd enjoyed talking to you.'

Adam shook his head in wry self-mockery. 'I
on't know why, I don't usually talk about my
ersonal feelings, but you were so much on my
1ind, I found myself telling him about our
lationship. He only made a few general comments
et suddenly the whole thing was very clear in my
1ind.'

A few general comments. Peggy wondered what
1ey had been. That perceptive old man had an
ncanny knack of pulling out the most telling
ords. She made a mental note to thank him next
me they met.

Adam's voice furred with emotion. 'You weren't
oing to come back to me, were you, Peggy?'

Her eyes ran slowly over the handsome face of the
1an she loved, a face which was inexpressibly dear
o her. 'I don't know, Adam. It would have been
erribly hard to stay away, but I thought you didn't
eally care about me. Not enough to . . .' She drew
1 a deep breath and gave him the bottom line. 'I

thought I was just another of your live-in ladies.

'Not you, Peggy.' His other hand came up gent
to cup her cheek and there was something beautifu
ly melting in his eyes. 'I love you. I've never sai
that to any other woman and tomorrow I'm going t
tell the whole damned world that you're the woma
I love . . . the woman I want to share the rest of m
life.'

Her arms flew up around his neck in an exultar
strangle-hold. 'Oh, Adam,' she breathed ecstatica
ly. 'I love you too. I've wanted to tell you so mar
times but I was scared you'd feel sort of burdened b
it.'

'Burdened! God almighty! You can lay th
burden on me any time.'

And he kissed her to show it was no burden at al
but a joy and a delight and a deep, wondrous feelin
which permeated the silence on the journey back t
Adam's home. Silence, but for one question.

'Did you talk to Robert about the song?' Pegg
asked.

'No. I didn't want to talk about it without yo
there,' Adam replied, and squeezed her hand t
express how much her presence meant to him.

Once in the private comfort of Adam's home
they were both able to express themselves wit
more fervour and the expression surpassed a
previous experiences.

The next morning Adam claimed the day as their
Lectures at the Institute had to be put aside fo
matters of prime importance. He took Peggy int
the city, supervised the fitting of a magnificer

olitaire diamond on the third finger of her left
and, insisted that he had the right of a fiancé to
uy her an elegant spring outfit, then drove her to
he television studios where they had first met.

He had arranged a special announcement ap-
earance on the Ross Elliot Show, and as the genial
alk-show host began his introductory spiel, Peggy's
ark eyes sparkled up at Adam, excitement and
appiness lending a brilliance which was as
azzling as the blueness of his.

'I'm sure you all remember the day when Adam
Gale met his blind date, Peggy Dean, on this show.
Yesterday there was a story about them in one of the
ewspapers. I've been informed by Adam Gale
imself that the story was not only distressing to
Peggy and her family, but basically incorrect in its
uppositions.

Ross Elliot paused, an old hand at the art of
elivering the punch-line. 'The truth is that Adam
net his proverbial Fate on this show, and he and
Peggy are to be married in the very near future. I'd
ike you all to put your hands together and let Peggy
nd Adam know that you wish them every
happiness as I welcome them back here today.'

The studio audience gave them a standing
vation as Adam led Peggy on to the set. Ross Elliot
ammed up the moment, lifting Peggy's hand up,
retending to examine the ring, then making sure it
lashed at the camera. The excitement gradually
ubsided as Ross saw Peggy and Adam settled into
rmchairs and resumed his own seat.

'So, Peggy won the war,' he declared
mischievously.

Adam laughed. 'I dont know about the war, Ross
but I sure won the spoils.' His beautiful blue eye
glowed their love at Peggy. 'And I'm never going t
let her go.'

Ross jiggled his eyebrows at the audience. 'Th
man is definitely serious.' Then he turned to Pegg
with a cajoling grin. 'I can't believe this courtshi
was all smooth sailing. Tell us the story, Peggy. I
certainly wasn't love at first sight.'

She smiled at Adam. 'Maybe at second sight.'

'I'm not too sure about that,' Adam retorted
feeling his cheek gingerly. 'We'd no sooner got of
this set last time when she whacked me across th
face for something I said that she didn't like. I te
you, Ross, she's a very strong-minded woman, and
damned near lost her a couple of times. I only fee
safe now because she's promised to marry me, an
she's a woman of her word.'

Peggy laughed and shook her head at him, bu
she knew he could only say such things because h
did feel safe with her.

'Is that true, Peggy?' Ross quizzed. 'Did yo
whack him one?'

'Oh yes, that's true,' she admitted. 'But then I fel
awful for losing my temper and he was very nic
about it.' She threw a teasing look at Adam. 'In fact
I think that was when I had my second sight and fel
in love with him.'

'And what about you, Adam? When did yo
decide that Peggy was the girl for you?' Ros
enquired with lively curiosity.

'When I looked out and saw her sitting in th
theatre on the première night of *Blind Date*. Jus

eing her there . . .' He smiled in remembrance. 'I
ink I gave the best performance of my life that
ight.'

'It was a great performance. I was there and I can
ouch for that,' Ross told his audience.

He asked several more provocative questions,
leverly and entertainingly drawing out the points
at Adam had wanted to impress on the public.
hen Ross congratulated them both again, shook
Adam's hand, kissed Peggy's cheek, and encour-
ged the viewers to call out benedictions on them as
ey left the set.

To Peggy's surprise they were waylaid by Gavin
n their walk out of the studios. 'Hey! Congratula-
ions, you two!' he beamed at them.

'Thanks, Gavin, but what are you doing here?'
eggy asked.

He shrugged. 'Ross said I could come over and
atch his operation. Just happened to be today.'

Go-getter Gavin, Peggy thought to herself but
he smiled at him, too happy to care what
dvantages he had over her, careerwise. 'Good for
ou.'

'And you,' he grinned. 'Didn't I tell you? Sex is
ower.'

'I hate to correct you, Gavin, but you're wrong,'
Adam said with firm authority, then smiled down at
eggy. 'Love is power.'

And on that triumphant note, Adam hugged
eggy to his side and walked her out into the
unshine . . . Spring sunshine which seemed to
romise them the most glorious, unforgettable
ummer of their lives.

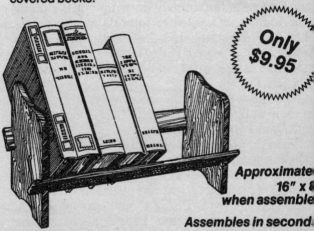

Can you keep a secret?

You can keep this one plus 4 free novels

GIFTS FROM THE HEART

MAIL-IN-OFFER

OFFER CERTIFICATE ✂

I have enclosed the required number of proofs of purchase from any specially marked "Gifts From The Heart" Harlequin romance book, plus cash register receipts and a check or money order payable to Harlequin Gifts From The Heart Offer, to cover postage and handling.

002

CHECK ONE	ITEM	# OF PROOFS OF PURCHASE	POSTAGE & HANDLING FEE
	01 Brass Picture Frame	2	$ 1.00
	02 Heart-Shaped Candle Holders with Candles	3	$ 1.00
	03 Heart-Shaped Keepsake Box	4	$ 1.00
	04 Gold-Plated Heart Pendant	5	$ 1.00
	05 Collectors' Doll Limited quantities available	12	$ 2.75

NAME _____

STREET ADDRESS _____ APT. # _____

CITY _____ STATE _____ ZIP _____

Mail this certificate, designated number of proofs of purchase (inside back page) and check or money order for postage and handling to:

Gifts From The Heart, P.O. Box 4814
Reidsville, N. Carolina 27322-4814

NOTE THIS IMPORTANT OFFER'S TERMS

Requests must be postmarked by May 31, 1988. Only proofs of purchase from specially marked "Gifts From The Heart" Harlequin books will be accepted. This certificate plus cash register receipts and a check or money order to cover postage and handling must accompany your request and may not be reproduced in any manner. Offer void where prohibited, taxed or restricted by law. LIMIT ONE REQUEST PER NAME, FAMILY, GROUP, ORGANIZATION OR ADDRESS. Please allow up to 8 weeks after receipt of order for shipment. Offer only good in the U.S.A. Hurry—Limited quantities of collectors' doll available. Collectors' dolls will be mailed to first 15,000 qualifying submitters. All other submitters will receive 12 free previously unpublished Harlequin books and a postage & handling refund.

OFFER-1RP

PAMELA BROWNING

...is fireworks on the green at the Fourth of July and prayers said around the Thanksgiving table. It is the dream of freedom realized in thousands of small towns across this great nation.

But mostly, the Heartland is its people. People who care about and help one another. People who cherish traditional values and give to their children the greatest gift, the gift of love.

American Romance presents HEARTLAND, an emotional trilogy about people whose memories, hopes and dreams are bound up in the acres they farm.

HEARTLAND...the story of America.

Don't miss these heartfelt stories: American Romance #237 SIMPLE GIFTS (March), #241 FLY AWAY (April), and #245 HARVEST HOME (May).

HRT-1

GIFTS FROM THE HEART

from *Harlequin*

FREE BY MAIL With proofs of purchase
plus postage and handling

A. Hand-polished solid brass picture frame 1-5/8" × 1-3/8" with 2 proofs of purchase.

B. Individually handworked, pair of heart-shaped glass candle holders (2" diameter), 6" candles included, with 3 proofs of purchase.

C. Heart-shaped porcelain keepsake box (1" high) with delicate flower motif with 4 proofs of purchase.

D. Radiant gold-plated heart pendant on 16" chain with complimentary satin pouch with 5 proofs of purchase.

E. Beautiful collectors' doll with genuine porcelain face, hands and feet, and a charming heart appliqué on dress with 12 proofs of purchase. Limited quantities available. See offer terms.

HERE IS HOW TO GET YOUR FREE GIFTS

Send us the required number of proofs of purchase (below) of specially marked "Gifts From The Heart" Harlequin books and cash register receipts with the Offer Certificate (available in the back pages) properly completed, plus a check or money order (do not send cash) payable to Harlequin Gifts From The Heart Offer. We'll RUSH you your specified gift. Hurry—Limited quantities of collectors' doll available. See offer terms.